everyday
angel

New Beginnings

VICTORIA SCHWAB

everyday angel

New Beginnings

SCHOLASTIC INC.

To Carla, for always knowing how to lift my spirits.

ISBN 978-0-545-68443-9

12 11 10 9 8 7 6 5 4   14 15 16 17 18/0

Printed in the U.S.A.   40
This edition first printing, January 2014

Book design by Yaffa Jaskoll

chapter 1

GABBY

"Ready . . ." said Gabby, stretching. "Set . . ."

She got halfway through the word *go!* before her brother, Marco, took off.

"Cheater!" she shouted, sprinting after him.

The woods behind their house grew up instead of out; trees densely piled onto hills like the one Gabby and Marco Torres were racing up now. Marco was older by three years, but Gabby was quick on her feet and knew the shortcuts. Marco always took the paths, but Gabby climbed the un-paths, the places where roots and rocks made stairs up the side of the forest.

"Come on, Gabs!" His voice rang out through the trees. "Keep up!"

Her lungs burned as she ran, twigs snapping under her shoes. She had never beaten him to the top. Even when he didn't cheat. But maybe today . . . She caught a glimpse of his bright blue T-shirt cutting between trees, and she sped up. She was so focused on catching him that she didn't see the fallen branch until it snagged her sneaker and sent her stumbling to her hands and knees on the damp ground. She sprung back up, but by then, she'd lost him.

His laughter rang out, and she sprinted on until she burst through the tree line, breathless, and grinning. "Marco!" she called. "I won!"

But Marco wasn't there. She stood at the top of the hill, catching her breath, waiting for her brother to get there and give her some line about *letting* her win. She waited, and waited, and waited.

"Marco?" she called nervously, looking around the field.

The hill was suddenly too still and too dark. The laughter that had followed her through the woods before reached her again, but it was twisted and wrong. It was her brother's voice, but he wasn't laughing anymore, not at all.

He was coughing.

Gasping.

Choking.

And that's when Gabby woke up.

She wasn't standing on a hilltop but slouched in a stiff hospital chair next to a bed. In the bed, Marco was doubled over, coughing. A nurse rubbed his back with one hand and adjusted his IV with the other.

"Hey there . . . Gabby," Marco said between coughs. "Sorry . . . didn't mean . . . to wake you."

"It's okay," Gabby mumbled, rubbing her forehead. "Bad dream. Are you all right?" she asked as Marco settled back against his pillow, his face flushed.

"Right as rain," he said, still struggling for air. "Don't tell anyone, though," he whispered loudly. "I don't want them to kick me out." The nurse toying with the machine laughed a little, and Gabby managed a thin smile. Marco was always joking.

But the coughing fit had clearly winded him. He looked tired. These days, he always looked tired. Gabby knew it was because of *the bad*.

When the doctors explained Marco's condition to Gabby, they didn't call the sickness by its proper name. They referred to it only as *the bad*, as if she didn't know how to search the Internet and find out what *the bad* really was. Now she knew the proper term — *osteosarcoma* — but still found herself thinking of it as *the bad*. Not because she wanted to dumb it down, or make it seem smaller, but because it was easier for her to picture the thing attacking her brother's body not as a many-syllabled word but as a monster.

Monsters could be fought. And Marco was fighting.

He looked at her and frowned his big-brother frown and said, "You were supposed to go home last night."

Gabby glanced down at her crumpled clothes and thought about how wrong it felt to call the new apartment *home*. *Home* was a place in the country with wooded hills and laughter and a healthy big brother. A place Gabby seemed to get back to only in her dreams. And as bad as the hospital was, the apartment was worse. It was a ghostly shell, empty and dark — their mom spent every free minute in the hospital with Marco.

"I like it better here," Gabby said, picking up the cheerful tone he'd dropped. "And the food's good. Way better than Mom's."

Marco chuckled carefully. "That may be true . . ." he said, letting out a sigh, "but you can't keep sleeping here. Not with school starting tomorrow."

Not just school, thought Gabby. *A* new *school.*

Grand Heights Middle School.

The thought of starting seventh grade there filled her with a mixture of fear and hope. When Marco had first gotten sick last year, everything had changed. Not just for him but for Gabby, too. Suddenly she couldn't go anywhere without being smothered by everybody's concern. Teachers, classmates, friends — their pity became like a low wall around her life. People wanted to look over and say hi, but the wall stopped them from getting too close. That was the weird thing about sickness. Even when it wasn't contagious, people kept their distance.

Even Alice and Beth, who were Gabby's closest friends, started acting strange around her. They got weird and quiet and went out of their way to be polite, and she hated it.

When Marco got transferred to a new hospital in a new city over the summer, Gabby had almost been relieved to leave.

Grand Heights Middle School would be filled with strangers, but it would also be a fresh start. Maybe she didn't have to be that girl with the sick brother.

Maybe she could just be Gabrielle Torres.

Marco cleared his throat. He was looking at her expectantly, and Gabby realized she'd gone quiet. She did that sometimes.

"*¿Dónde estás?*" he asked. *Where are you?* But what he meant was, *Where is your head? Where have you gone? Come back.*

"Sorry, I'm here," she said, blinking. And then she remembered. "Oh, hey, I got you something."

Gabby fetched a plastic shopping bag filled with school supplies from under her chair. She had picked them out herself. Her mom hadn't been able to take her shopping, but the mall, like the apartment, like the school, like *everything else,* was in walking distance from the hospital. Gabby dug through the bag until she found the blue-and-white-striped notebook and pen. "For your homeschooling," she said.

"Hospital-schooling," corrected Marco. He was fifteen, and should have been starting tenth grade at Grand Heights High. Instead, he'd be here with a tutor.

Gabby dropped a fresh pack of colored paper on the pale hospital bed. "And this is for the rest of the time," she said.

Marco's eyes lit up. He was an *expert* paper-airplane maker, and they spent the next half hour folding the paper into planes to throw from his third-floor window and into the parking lot below. Gabby had just succeeded in landing her third purple plane on a white minivan roof — Marco cheering her on — when the door opened behind them.

"Gabrielle Torres," said a quiet voice with mock scorn. "Are you letting your brother have too much fun?"

She turned to see Marco's new friend, Henry, coming into the room in his wheelchair. Henry reminded her of paper. Not the rich, colorful kind that she and Marco had been making into airplanes, but a worn and faded white. He was pale to start with — she'd seen photos from when he was a kid — and paler from being sick, his hair a watery blond, and his eyes a gentle, washed-out blue.

Gabby shook her head, and Henry tsked.

"Didn't he tell you," Henry went on, wheeling himself up to the bed, "what'll happen if he has too much fun here?"

"They'll kick him out?" ventured Gabby.

"Exactly!" said Henry, knocking his knees against the metal bed rail. "You don't want him to get kicked out, do you? Who would entertain *me*?"

"*You* could have too much fun," offered Gabby. "Then they'd kick you out, too."

Henry's smile turned sad at the edges. "Nah, they like me too much to let me go." His eyes fell to the plastic bag on the bed. "What have we here?"

"School supplies," said Marco. "Gabby starts tomorrow."

"Wow," said Henry with a soft, soundless laugh. "School, already? Time really does fly when you're having fun."

"Do you miss it?" asked Gabby. Henry was the same age as Marco, but she knew he'd been sick a lot longer, and a lot worse, and wondered how long it had been since he'd hefted a backpack onto his shoulder, or heard a shrill class bell.

"Nah," he said with a shrug. "Best part of being here is I don't have to go to school."

7

Gabby didn't believe him. She could see it tucked away in Henry's eyes, how much he missed being a normal teenage boy, even if normal meant school and homework and chores. She could see it starting in Marco's eyes, too, even though their mom was still dragging him through the motions so he wouldn't fall too far behind. Henry looked as if he might never catch back up. The thought shot like a pang through Gabby's chest, but she didn't have a chance to dwell on Henry's condition, because Marco started coughing again.

Gabby winced as two nurses appeared out of the hospital cracks, one doing her best to get Marco settled, while the other wheeled Henry away. The bag of school supplies tumbled off the bed, and Gabby was on her hands and knees, trying to gather up the pens and notebooks, when her mom rushed in.

"What is it?" asked Mrs. Torres, only adding to the commotion. "What's wrong? Marco? Are you all right? How long has this been going on?"

"He'll be fine," urged a nurse, but her calm somehow made Gabby's mom more flustered, and Mrs. Torres gathered up the colored papers on the bed in a single sweep and dumped them into a chair. She muttered to Gabby in Spanish

8

about making a mess as she rubbed circles on Marco's back to help him breathe.

Gabby backed out of the room and into the hall. She slumped against the wall beside the door, every muscle in her body tense, as if she'd been the one coughing. She looked down and realized she was still holding some of the school supplies: a pretty journal with music notes and a handful of pens. Through the door, she could hear the scene quieting, but Marco's cough echoed in her head and she couldn't bring herself to go back in — she'd probably just be in the way. So she stayed put in the corridor.

Most of the halls on this floor were painted yellow or green, but this one was blue. Gabby liked the color because it made her feel like a little piece of outside had wandered in. She'd spent a lot of time in hospitals, and so often their pale walls and fluorescent lights reminded her that she was definitely *not* outside. Now, if she stared at the wall and let her eyes unfocus, she could *almost* believe she was staring at the sky on a nice day, warm and sunny and blue.

chāpter 2

ARIA

Outside the hospital, it was a cloudy day.

No blue sky. No sunlight. No shade. So it was strange when a shadow formed in the middle of the parking lot.

It started as a blot and spread across the pavement. Even if there *had* been a sun out, casting shadows, there was no source nearby — no car, no lamppost, and certainly no person — to cast this particular one.

The impossible shadow grew until it was roughly the size and shape of a twelve-year-old girl with long, wavy hair. And once it was done growing, the shadow *changed*. It went from dark to blinding white, as if a hundred lights had been turned on somewhere deep inside of it. And out of the light came a girl.

In one slow, fluid motion, like coming up through water, the girl rose out of the mark on the ground. And when she was standing on top of the girl-shaped puddle of white, the blinding light inside went off like a switch.

The girl looked down at her shadow approvingly.

"Nice work," she said to it.

The shadow seemed pleased, fidgeting happily beneath her feet. The girl looked around, marveling at the fact she was *here* — even if *here* was a hospital parking lot on a cloudy afternoon — and a thrill ran through her at the thought of being somewhere.

Being *someone*.

There was only one problem.

The girl in the parking lot didn't know who she was.

That is to say, she knew *what* she was, but this was her first day as a *who*. And now that she was a *who*, she couldn't help but wonder what type of *who* she was. She brought her hands up in front of her face, as if they would tell her, and in a way they did. A blue bracelet circled her wrist, bare except for a pendant with a name carved on it in small, delicate script.

Aria.

She tested the word on her tongue a few times and liked it.

"My name is Aria," she told her shadow. It gave the slightest nod.

And then she looked down at herself for the first time. She was delighted to find she was wearing a green shirt and a white skirt with pockets and a pair of bright blue leggings that ran right into her sneakers. The laces on the shoes were white, until Aria — she really did like the name — decided she'd rather have purple ones. As soon as she thought it, color began to seep down the shoestrings, turning them violet.

Aria smiled and caught up a chunk of her hair, holding it in front of her eyes so she could see the color. Even in the gray day, flecks of coppery red glittered in the brown strands.

Delightful, thought Aria. She let the strands slip from her fingers as her eyes (a greeny blue, even though she didn't know that yet) drifted up to the white building that loomed in front of her. It was very large, and she bit her lip and wondered how she would find whoever she was looking for in a place that big.

Well, thought Aria decisively, *one thing at a time.*

First, the shadow.

She couldn't just run off and leave it there in the lot (well, she *could,* but that would be strange). So she located its head behind her, and its feet in front of her, and then she took two small steps forward so that her shoes nested cleanly into the shoes of the shadow instead of standing on its stomach. Aria then rolled from her heels to her toes and back a few times until she was sure the shadow had stuck, moving when she moved, stopping when she stopped, and behaving in all ways like a perfectly normal shadow.

Once she was satisfied that it wouldn't come loose, Aria smoothed her skirt, tucked a strand of hair behind her ear, and made her way to the hospital.

A dozen steps led to a set of glass doors, and a man and a woman were sitting halfway up the stairs, huddled side by side despite the warm day. The woman seemed upset — *very* upset — and Aria wanted to help. But she couldn't. She *shouldn't.*

Because there was no blue smoke.

Aria knew she wasn't supposed to get involved unless she saw the blue smoke. It was the reason she was here. The smoke would show her the person who needed her help. The fact the shadow had brought her to the hospital meant someone inside would be marked by it. The people on the steps weren't. As sad as they seemed, they must not need the kind of help that Aria — or someone like her — could provide.

Aria reached the revolving glass doors, and stopped. Not just because the door itself was strange and vaguely concerning. But because there, in the glass, she saw something for the first time. Herself.

It was one thing, looking at the pieces — hands, shoes, skirt, hair — but it was such another, bigger, better thing to see herself as a whole. Well, *almost* whole. Her eyes hovered on the empty space above her shoulders, the place where her wings should be . . . *would* be, once she'd earned them.

Just then the revolving doors jerked into motion, and Aria jumped back as a man came through the turning portal. He left the glass spinning, Aria's reflection coming and going and coming again. She darted forward, jumped back out on the other side, and found herself inside the hospital.

The lobby was filled with people, some in white coats, moving briskly, and some in regular clothes, slumped in chairs. Others still were pacing or waiting or talking to one another or to no one. Aria scanned the crowd, but she didn't see any smoke.

"Good afternoon," said a woman behind the desk. "How can I help you?"

Aria approached the desk. "I'm just trying to find someone."

"Who are you looking for?" asked the woman.

"Oh, I don't know," said Aria brightly. "I haven't found them yet." The woman frowned, but before she could say anything, Aria smiled and added, "Don't worry. I'll know them when I see them."

And with that she set off down the hall on the left.

If the woman had been looking closely, she might have noticed that each of the fluorescent lights overhead grew a little brighter as Aria passed beneath them. Or that the scuffs on the linoleum faded under her shoes, leaving the floor clean and new. But she didn't notice. No one did. They were small changes, the kind you sensed but couldn't put your finger on. Aria made the world a little nicer just by being in it.

She explored two floors in search of the smoke — scanning halls, peering through windows and around doors — until she stumbled upon a common room. Several children clustered around a TV, a few others sat around a table with a puzzle, but it was the boy by the window who caught her eye.

He was pale and blond and wreathed in smoke.

The dark plumes hung around him like a cloud as he stared out the window. But as Aria drew closer, she frowned. His smoke was the wrong color. Aria was meant to find *blue* smoke. But the cloud circling the boy's shoulders was a dark, bruised purple. Almost black.

He was definitely marked, but not for Aria.

"Henry," said a voice, and the boy by the window looked up as a nurse carried a cup of water over to his wheelchair.

Aria wondered why Henry was here, and why he was shrouded in such a grim cloud. She looked around, searching for someone like her, maybe someone with a charm bracelet to match that particular shade of purple-black smoke. But no one stood out. In fact, Aria was the only person in the common room who didn't look like she belonged there.

Until another girl came in. She was about Aria's size, with warm, tan skin and rich, dark hair. But what caught Aria's attention wasn't the girl's skin or her hair or the notebook she was clutching to her chest. It was the blue smoke swirling around her shoulders.

Smoke the exact same color as Aria's bracelet.

The girl wove absently through the tables and chairs, lost in her own thoughts, and flopped down onto a couch in the corner. Aria hesitated. She'd been so focused on finding the smoke, she didn't know what to do now. So she stood there, watching, hoping the girl would give some clue as to what was wrong.

The girl didn't seem *sick*, not like the other kids in the common room. But that didn't surprise Aria. After all, the smoke had nothing to do with sickness. It marked a person only if Aria could help them, and she couldn't help sickness. She wasn't a healer. (She didn't even know if those existed.) Aria was just . . . Aria. And whatever was wrong with the blue-smoke girl, Aria was pretty sure she wouldn't figure it out by standing there. Plus she was beginning to feel awkward about staring. So she took a deep breath, walked up to the girl on the couch, and said hello.

chapter 3

GABBY

Gabby had been squinting up at the ceiling, trying to decide if the lights in the room had gotten brighter, when someone said, "Hello!"

She looked over to find a girl perched on the opposite edge of the couch. The girl had coppery hair and bright blue leggings and a cheerful smile. The thing about hospitals was that few people smiled like that. They grimaced with worry, or pursed their lips with pity, and on occasion they beamed with relief, but they rarely seemed *cheerful*.

"Hi," said Gabby cautiously.

"What's your name?" asked the girl. She looked like she was Gabby's age. There were a few other twelve-year-olds here, but all of them were sick. In fact, Gabby hadn't seen a girl her age who *wasn't* sick all summer.

"Gabrielle Torres," she said, then added, "Most people call me Gabby. You?"

The girl's smile brightened, as if the question thrilled her.

"My name's Aria." She held up her hand and Gabby could see the name etched into a metal pendant on the girl's charm bracelet. "See?"

Gabby nodded. It was a pretty name, one she hadn't really heard before.

A beat of silence fell between them. Gabby realized Aria was staring at her. Gabby stared back.

"So . . ." said Aria. She tapped her fingers on her knee, her gaze wandering over the room like she was searching for something — anything — to say. When her eyes found the far green wall, her lips curved up.

"What's your favorite color?" she asked.

Gabby's eyebrows rose. People asked a lot of questions in hospitals — *How are you feeling? Can you rate your pain? Do you need anything?* But *What's your favorite color?* wasn't one of them. She shrugged.

"I'm not sure," Gabby said. She knew Marco's favorite — green — and she knew what hers *used* to be — purple — but it had been so long since she thought about something silly like that. With so many big questions out there, how could she care about something stupid like colors? The black music notes on her notebook stared up at her from their white background, not helping.

"Don't worry," said Aria. "I'm not sure, either."

"Really?"

Aria nodded. "Really. Or at least, I can't decide. I see one color and I think that might be it, my favorite, but then I see another and I change my mind. It's so hard to pick only one. Like my laces," she said, gesturing to the shoestrings, which were now hot pink. "I've changed them twice so far today."

Gabby almost smiled. Aria was weird.

"There is one color I don't like," admitted Aria. "The color they've painted the hospital steps. That sad gray. It's almost like a noncolor. It's . . ."

"Sickly," offered Gabby.

"Exactly," said Aria, shaking her head.

Something moved at the edge of Gabby's sight, and she turned to see the nurse wheeling Henry away. Gabby waved and Henry waved back.

Aria watched him go, too, with a strange look on her face.

"That's Henry," said Gabby. "Do you know him?"

After a pause, Aria shook her head. "Not really. Why is he here?"

Gabby smiled sadly. "If you ask him, he'll say it's because the doctors like him too much to let him go." Her smile fell. Wouldn't it be nice, to live in a world where that was true? "He's really sick," she added. "I don't know if he's going to get better."

"The smoke," Aria said to herself. "It's really dark."

Gabby frowned. "What are you talking about?"

Aria's attention snapped back to her. "Nothing. I just . . . I hope he gets better."

"Me too," said Gabby.

She squinted at Aria. What was she doing in the hospital? Unlike Gabby, she didn't wear the battle scars of those bound to the sick. No bags under her eyes from spending nights here. No cringing at the sound of a distant cough. Nothing tired or worn or tense about her. In fact, she radiated health.

"Do you have family being treated here?" asked Gabby.

Aria shook her head.

"Then why are you here?" asked Gabby, hoping she didn't sound rude.

Aria looked down at her pink laces. "I'm just here to help."

"Oh," said Gabby, "so you're like a volunteer?"

Aria hesitated, scrunched up her brow, and then nodded decidedly. "Yes, like that."

"I didn't know they let people our age work at the hospital," said Gabby.

Aria hesitated again. "Well," she said, "you have to start sometime. What about you?"

"What about me?" asked Gabby.

"Do you have family here?"

Now it was Gabby's turn to hesitate. She'd said more in the last few minutes than she had in days. It felt nice to talk to someone, and she hated the idea of the girl's smile turning tight with pity. But it wasn't like Gabby could hide Marco's sickness, not when she was *in* his hospital.

"My brother's here," Gabby finally replied. "He's sick."

Gabby braced herself for the *I'm sorry*, but Aria simply nodded and asked, "Is it bad, like Henry?"

Gabby looked down at her notebook. "It's different."

Marco's *bad* had started last year on a soccer field. At first they'd thought the pain in his leg and hip was just another growth spurt — he was tall for fourteen — but it kept getting worse. And then one day when he and Gabby were racing up the wooded hill behind their house, he'd had to stop, he couldn't make it to the top. And they took him to the doctor and found out that it wasn't normal, wasn't natural. The tests confirmed it. A series of tumors — such an ugly word, like a kind of beast — were attacking the bones in Marco's left leg. From his knee all the way up through his hip.

And they were growing.

Fast.

In a matter of weeks, the Torres family's life had been overtaken by *the bad*. Marco began an aggressive treatment plan to stop the tumors from spreading. The doctors explained that they had to shrink the tumors first. So that when they operated on Marco, it would be easier to remove them all.

Nothing about the treatment had been easy. But Marco had done it. He'd fought his way this far. And now it was time to operate, or it *should* be, but . . .

"Gabby?" pressed Aria.

"We're waiting," she said, willing herself to say the words out loud. "We moved here over the summer so my brother, Marco, could have an operation, but a couple weeks ago he got sick. Not a big kind of sick. A small kind, a bad cold, but still. They keep putting his surgery on hold. And now we're waiting."

The truth was, every time Marco coughed, every time his temperature went up or he slept too long, the panic in Gabby's chest got worse. What if they *couldn't* clear him for surgery? What if *the bad* came back before they could operate? What if —

23

"It's okay," said Aria softly, as if she could hear Gabby's worried thoughts. And Aria's tone did make Gabby relax, just a little bit.

"I'm starting school tomorrow," Gabby went on, "and I'm worried about Marco, but there's this part of me that can't wait to get away from here. When I'm here all I can think about — all *anyone* can think about — is my brother's sickness. But when I go to school at least I can pretend for a little while that things are okay. Normal. That I'm not just the sister of a kid with cancer."

The moment she spoke those words, Gabby felt horrible. She wasn't ashamed of Marco or his illness. But if she could have anything in the world, it would be for him to get healthy. It wasn't Marco's fault he was sick. *This is why I should keep my mouth shut*, Gabby told herself. Half of the time her thoughts didn't seem important. The other half of the time she hated herself for even thinking them.

Gabby started to take back what she'd said, when Aria said, "That makes sense."

"It does?" asked Gabby.

Aria nodded. "Sure. Your brother's sick. You're not."

Gabby found herself nodding. "I know it's wrong," she said, "but I'm just tired of . . . I don't know. . . ." She fumbled for the words. "In a hospital, the only people who matter are the ones in the beds. But when someone you care about is sick, you get sick, too, in a different way. . . ."

Just then she heard a text come in on her phone. She dug it out of her pocket.

"What was that?" asked Aria as the phone made another chirping sound.

"My mom," said Gabby, getting to her feet. "I have to go." She couldn't believe she'd told the girl so much, but it felt good. "Thanks," she added.

"For what?" asked Aria.

"For listening."

Aria smiled. "That's what I'm here for."

At that, Gabby's heart sank a little. Sitting there, talking to Aria, she'd felt special, important. She'd totally forgotten that Aria was a volunteer at the hospital. It was probably just her job to make people feel better.

"I'll see you around," said Gabby, quickly turning to go.

Aria shoved her hands in the pockets of her skirt, and smiled. "You will."

chapter 4

ARIA

Aria watched Gabby walk away, the blue smoke swirling around her shoulders. She waited a moment, then hopped up from the couch and followed. Gabby had vanished around a corner, but thin tendrils of smoke trailed behind her, and soon enough Aria caught sight of her near the end of a pale blue hall. She was standing outside a door, staring in.

Aria hesitated. She wanted to go over to Gabby, but she thought it would seem strange, her showing up so soon after they'd said good-bye. Better if she could stay with Gabby for a little while without the girl knowing. If only she could watch *unseen*.

Was that possible? Aria wondered, looking down at her hands. Some things she knew with absolute clarity — what she was, what she was meant to do, what she *couldn't* do, what she *mustn't* do. But what she *could* do and what she *should* do, those things were muddy, blurred.

Only one way to find out, thought Aria.

Staring down at her hands, she willed herself to disappear. At first nothing happened. And then, between one blink and the next, she was gone. She'd expected something slow and spreading, the way color did through her laces, but she didn't bleed out of sight. She just vanished.

She could still feel the linoleum beneath her shoes, but there were no shoes to *see.* Aria shivered a little. She didn't like it. What if she couldn't undo it? She wanted to undo it!

And just like that, she was there again, green top and blue leggings and pink laces in the hall.

Aria sighed with relief.

What an unpleasant thing, being invisible. It made her *feel* less real. But it was necessary. And now that Aria knew she could undo the illusion, she took a deep breath, made herself invisible again, and joined Gabby in front of the door.

Gabby was peering in through a glass insert, and as Aria looked over her shoulder, she could see what Gabby saw in the room. A boy in a bed.

It had to be Gabby's brother, Marco. He was propped up against several pillows, sleeping. He wasn't what Aria had pictured, not frail like that other boy, Henry. No, Marco was broad-shouldered, with dark brown hair and golden skin.

Gabby was about to turn the knob when a woman called to her from down the hall.

"Gabrielle," said the woman, her voice tense. She had a crease between her eyebrows and circles under her eyes, and she looked like an older, sadder version of Gabby. Aria guessed that she was her mother.

"Where have you been?" she asked.

Gabby's hand fell away from the door. "I was wandering."

"Well, you've had *me* wandering all over this place looking for you."

"I'm sorry," said Gabby automatically. "I was just trying to stay out of the way." She turned back toward the door. "How's Marco?"

"Sleeping, again," answered her mom, softening. "I'm going to stay with him awhile longer."

"I can stay, too."

Mrs. Torres shook her head. "I want you to go home."

"It isn't home," muttered Gabby under her breath.

Her mom tutted. "Don't talk back. Just go." Gabby's shoulders slumped. "And if I'm not there by nine thirty," added her mom, "I want you *in bed*."

28

"But you'll be there in the morning, right?" asked Gabby. "To wish me luck?"

Mrs. Torres's brow crinkled in confusion, and then her eyes widened. "Yes, yes, of course," she said. "Big day, *mija*. You have everything you need? All your supplies?"

Gabby nodded. "I think so."

"Seventh grade," said her mom, voice tight. "When did you grow up?"

It was a small question, said more to herself than her daughter. Aria saw the pain in Gabby's face, but the girl only shrugged and said, "I need to grab my things." She slipped silently into Marco's room.

Aria stayed in the hall with Gabby's mom. Aria could see the question flickering like a light behind the woman's eyes — *When did you grow up?* And for a moment it was like Gabby's mom had looked at her daughter and actually *seen* her. Aria willed Gabby's mom to hold on to that glimmer, but a second later Mrs. Torres's pocket gave a shrill double-beep. By the time she dug out the phone, the glimmer was fading. By the time she answered, the glimmer was gone.

She started talking rapidly in Spanish and was halfway down the hall with her cell pressed to her ear by the time Gabby reappeared, shopping bag in hand.

Aria watched Gabby watch her mother. Gabby's mouth was pressed into a small, sad line. Aria realized that that moment when Mrs. Torres saw her daughter was just that. A *moment*. And Aria could tell from the disappointed look on Gabby's face that it was a rare moment.

Even though Gabby was trying to hold it together in the hall, Aria could tell that she was upset. Hurt. And suddenly, Aria understood something.

Gabby wanted to be noticed.

She wanted to be *seen*.

And Aria was the one who was going to help her. She didn't know exactly how, but she would find a way. It was why she was here. It was her job. Her purpose.

Gabby started off down the hall, and Aria followed. Down the elevator and through the lobby and past the revolving doors — Aria nearly collided with the glass because she couldn't *see* herself in it — and down those horrible gray steps.

Aria paused to cast a last glance back at the hospital. The sun was sinking, the low light glinting against the building, making it look sharp, unwelcoming. When she turned back, Gabby had gotten a ways ahead, and Aria had to run to catch up.

As she reached her side, she noticed something.

Gabby had started to hum.

It was nothing more than a small, wandering melody, but it was lovely. Aria didn't know if all people sounded as nice when they sang, and she was about to try when she remembered her current invisible state. So she kept her mouth shut and listened, the sound filling her with warmth. The melody had an effect on Gabby, too. As she hummed, her shoulders began to loosen, the strain going out of her face.

And then Gabby came to a stop in front of an apartment building and looked up. The humming trailed off, the easy song replaced by heavy silence. Gabby took a deep breath, climbed the steps to the front door, and went inside. Aria moved to follow, but by the time she got to the door, it had fallen shut again. When she tried the handle, it didn't move. Aria frowned. It hadn't been locked. Gabby had gone right in (she could hear her fading footsteps), but when Aria tried it again, it wouldn't budge. She *willed* the door to open, the way she'd willed herself invisible, the way she'd willed her shoclaces to change colors.

But it didn't work.

Weird, she thought. It should be so simple, opening something that's closed, certainly easier than disappearing.

31

But Aria couldn't do it. Was she not strong enough yet? Or was it somehow breaking a rule?

Aria gazed up at the building, which was eight stories tall and five windows wide, and wondered which apartment belonged to Gabby. She thought about going for a walk, or making her way back to the hospital. But now that she'd found the blue smoke, found Gabby, it was like a thread connected them, a thread with only so much length, and Aria felt an uncomfortable tightness in her chest at the thought of testing its reach.

Overhead, a light turned on. Four floors up and one window over. When Aria squinted, she could almost see a curl of blue smoke up there. Gabby's apartment.

Aria looked around. All she needed was a way *up*. The simple answer would be to fly, but Aria didn't know if she could do that without wings. She closed her eyes and tried to picture herself airborne, but when she opened her eyes, she was still standing on the ground. Fine then. If she couldn't fly, she would climb.

The moment she thought it, a ladder appeared, simple and wooden and running all the way from the grass to the apartment roof eight floors up.

Strange powers, thought Aria as she brought her hand to a lower rung and began to climb. Up four stories she went —

she wasn't afraid of heights — until she reached Gabby's window.

Gabby was nowhere to be seen, but Aria could hear humming and the opening and closing of drawers in the kitchen.

She took one hand off the ladder and tried to open the window. It wouldn't budge. Aria made a small, indignant sound. A ladder! A ladder, out of nothing, and she still couldn't manage to open something closed! It *had* to be a rule.

Aria mentally added *cannot trespass* to the short list of things she knew she couldn't do, right under *cannot heal the sick* and *cannot fly (I think)*. And then she sighed, wrapped her arms around the ladder, and tried to decide what she *could* do. She couldn't — well, she *shouldn't* — just stand there outside the window all night. It was uncomfortable, and probably a little creepy, even if she was invisible.

She either needed to climb down, or climb up.

The setting sun was streaking colors across the sky, and Aria wanted to be closer to it, so she chose up. The ladder ended just at the lip of the roof, and Aria swung her leg over. Then she stood on top of the apartment building, feeling as if she were on top of the world.

She finally allowed herself to become visible again. She looked down at her hands and let out a relieved sigh, surprised at how much effort it had taken to be *in*visible. Every moment she couldn't see herself she felt the need to *remind* herself she was still there, still real. She spent a few moments making sure every bit of her was back, from legs and arms to laces — still pink — and her bracelet.

In the fading light, she examined the blue circling her wrist and noticed something she hadn't before. There were small loops woven through the material, rings where charms could be added. Three of them. Her heart jumped. Was that how many people she needed to help? Was that how she would earn her wings?

Aria's spirits lifted at the thought. Three people. True, she hadn't even succeeded in helping *one* person yet, but she would. She would help Gabby get rid of her smoke, and she'd be a full step closer to a pair of wings.

She turned her attention back to the sky. It was mesmerizing, the way it changed. She watched the oranges slide into pinks and then deeper purples, shifting and then fading into darkness. The sky made her think of Gabby. Gabby, who was fading, too, becoming invisible even though she didn't want to be.

Marco's sickness was loud and bright and big enough to make everything else feel small. It wasn't his fault. It wasn't anyone's fault. But it was time for Gabby to find her light. Find her voice.

Aria smiled. She couldn't wait for tomorrow.

Because tomorrow, Gabby would go to school.

And Aria would be with her.

chāpter 5

GABBY

"Hello?" Gabby called out, even though she knew the apartment was empty. Her *abuela* — her mother's mother — always said that when you came home, you had to let any ghosts know you were there. Gabby's grandmother always stomped her feet on the mat and clapped her weathered hands and made a racket every time she entered an empty room.

Gabby didn't believe in ghosts, and even if she did, she thought a *hello* was probably enough. Still, as she made her way through the apartment, she went back to humming. She sang to herself as she kicked off her shoes and dropped the bag of school supplies on the table.

Ghosts can't just come in, her *abuela* had added. *Not unless you let them.*

Are ghosts the only things? Gabby had asked.

Her *abuela* had tutted. *No*, mija. *Ghosts and monsters and angels and all those magic things, they all need your permission to come in.*

Why?

Why? Why? Because it's a rule. They have different rules than we do. Rules about right and wrong, and what is theirs and what is ours.

Her *abuela* was a strange, superstitious woman.

Don't ask why, just know it, her *abuela* had said. *And keep the door closed.*

Gabby wished her *abuela* had come with them — she still lived in their old town. She called all the time, but it wasn't the same. Gabby's mom said she was too old to travel, but Gabby knew the truth: she had a fear of hospitals — *too many go in, too few go out* — and would rather light candles for Marco from home.

Gabby found a frozen lasagna in the freezer and popped it in the microwave. She rapped her fingers on the counter, humming under the sound of the food cooking as her gaze wandered over the empty apartment. Her mom's room sat dark, practically unused, and down the hall Gabby's room was almost as lifeless. No dent in the wall from where Marco had thrown the ball and she'd failed to catch it. No scratch on the floor from where she'd tried to roller-skate indoors.

No notches on the doorframe from where they'd measured her height. Every time she flipped on the lights, she still found herself looking for those notches, as if one of the marks might have come with them from their old house. But none of them had.

Marco had a room, too, but he'd only slept in his bed one night between moving here and getting checked in at the hospital. Still, his was the only room that looked the least bit warm and welcoming, as if that would will him to get better faster, to come home. Not that this place felt like a home.

The microwave dinged. Because she couldn't eat and hum at the same time, Gabby turned on the TV, and a game show filled the apartment with hollow, high-pitched sound while she picked at the cheese on her lasagna.

"Marco?" Gabby called out, breathless from running.

He'd been right ahead of her. He'd been winning. And now he was gone.

She called his name again, hearing only the echo *Marco, Marco, Marco,* through the trees. Nothing else, not even his playful answer, *Polo, Polo, Polo.*

Gabby kept climbing up the hill, but when she got to the clearing at the top, it was empty. And quiet.

Fear began to claw at Gabby.

"Marco!" she cried out, but this time there wasn't even an echo. The world ate up the words and left only silence, thick and smothering, interrupted at last not by her brother's voice, but by a harsh, metallic alarm.

Gabby woke up, her throat and eyes burning as the alarm on her bedside table blared.

"Mom?" she called out, her voice shaky from the nightmare. No answer. She climbed out of bed and padded through the apartment, but there was no sign of her mother. She felt a wave of sadness, followed by panic.

Maybe there was a good reason her mom had stayed over at the hospital. Maybe something was wrong with Marco. Gabby went back to her room and grabbed her phone from her dresser. She hated that calling had become the easiest way to get her mom's attention.

It only rang twice before a voice said, "Hello?"

"Hey, Mom, it's me. I just wanted to make sure everything's okay."

"Yes, of course, why wouldn't . . ." She could hear her mom fumbling with the phone and pictured her looking at her watch. "Oh, *mija*, I'm so sorry. It got late and I was tired and I just closed my eyes for a moment. I was going to wake up early and come home in time."

"It's okay," said Gabby. "I just got worried."

"Do you want me to come home?" asked her mom.

Yes, thought Gabby. "No," she said. "It's fine."

She wanted her mom to insist, to say she was leaving, was already in the lot, was on her way. Instead, her mom said, "Okay."

Gabby's heart sank. Her mom was tuned to the slightest changes in Marco's mood, but Gabby felt like she had to shout if she wanted to be noticed. And she couldn't bring herself to do it. Couldn't find the voice.

"Have a great first day," added her mom.

"I'll try." A few tears escaped down Gabby's face before she could wipe them away. She hung up and shook her head, chiding herself.

This was seventh grade, not elementary school. She wasn't a little kid anymore. She didn't need her mom to see her off to class. This was her chance, her fresh start, and she couldn't let a silly little thing like the lack of a kiss on the cheek ruin it.

She focused on getting ready. Gabby stood at the mouth of her closet, surveying her wardrobe. Everything looked too bright, or too dull, or too big, or too tight. She hadn't gone shopping since before the move, had spent the summer in jeans and T-shirts (and hoodies, because the hospital was always cold). Now she was terrified that there would be some major trend at Grand Heights Middle that she didn't know about. Back home, Alice had always known the latest styles, while Beth chose not to care about clothes. Gabby fell somewhere in the middle. Now, she wondered: *Do the twelve-year-old girls here wear skirts? Headbands? Leggings?*

She thought of Aria's blue leggings from yesterday and dug around in a drawer until she found a pair of green ones so bright they must have been part of a Halloween costume. Reluctantly she tried them on under a frilly skirt. She chanced a look in the mirror and grimaced.

She looked ridiculous. Scrambling out of the outfit before anyone else could *ever* see, Gabby stared down at the clothes littering her bedroom floor. Again she wished her mom could be there to advise, and again she smothered the feeling. Seventh graders, she told herself, did not need parents to offer fashion input.

She finally settled on a version of her summer uniform: a pair of dark jeans, a red T-shirt with a scooped neck, and ballet flats. Not the most exciting outfit — she wasn't as fashion-forward as Alice, as carefree as Beth, or as bold as Aria — but it would do.

Gabby grabbed her backpack, walked out of her room, and took some money from an envelope tacked to the fridge labeled FOOD. She stomped her feet once by the front door to let any ghosts know she was leaving and marched downstairs. There was an orange cat on the front stoop, and she was just leaning down to pet it when she saw the school bus rounding the corner. She ran and reached the stop just as the bus did. Gabby took one last, deep breath, and climbed on board.

It was the first day, and the bus was only half full, but everyone on it seemed to know one another already. The kids huddled in groups, chatting about their summers. Gabby slid into a seat alone and looked out the window at her apartment building as the bus pulled away. She saw the orange cat stretching on the steps, but as her gaze drifted up the seven — no, eight — floors, she could have sworn she saw someone standing on the roof. A girl. She squinted, but a second later, when the bus rounded the corner, the figure was gone.

chapter 6

ARIA

Aria sat up abruptly.

She'd been lying on the rooftop, sprawled out on a few blankets. She'd summoned them, along with a pillow, the night before, the same way she had the ladder (it seemed summoning useful objects was firmly on the list of things she *could* do).

She hadn't fallen asleep exactly, but her mind had wandered off, and by the time she pulled it back the sun was shining and the air was cool and a small gray bird was pecking at her shadow. She shooed the bird away and got to her feet. It took a moment for her thoughts to collect, and when they did, they shaped into a single word.

Gabby.

And then another.

School.

Aria burst into motion, the pillow and blankets turning to fog and then to nothing around her feet as she hurried to the edge of the roof. She got there just in time to see Gabby stepping onto the school bus. Oh no.

With a last glance around the roof, Aria swung her leg over the edge of the ladder. But she'd made it down only a few rungs when someone cried out, and she froze.

A man on the sidewalk below was shouting up at her and waving his hands. At this height, she couldn't hear what he was saying, but one thing was clear. A twelve-year-old girl clinging to a ladder eight stories up was *not* normal.

The bus had turned the corner, taking Gabby with it, and the man was shouting frantically, and the front door of the building opened as a handful of other tenants came out to see what was going on, and in that moment Aria knew one thing: she needed to disappear.

It happened instantly, just as it had the day before, but then she'd been standing firmly on the ground and this time she'd been clinging to the ladder, and the sight of her fingers vanishing from the rungs made her lose her balance.

And in a moment of panic, Aria let go.

And she began to fall.

The man on the sidewalk stopped shouting, not because the other tenants were trying to calm him, but because he couldn't see Aria plummeting down. He couldn't see her at all.

But Aria was still there, and she was still falling very, very quickly toward the ground below.

Three seconds before she hit the ground, she realized very concretely that no, she could not fly.

Two seconds before she hit the ground, her shadow appeared beneath her, waiting.

And the second before she hit the ground, her shadow filled with brilliant, blinding light. And when Aria hit the ground, and the shadow, she fell straight through into the white.

The shadow took shape on the sidewalk across the street from the school.

If the hundreds of sixth, seventh, and eighth graders had been looking back at their parents' cars and the school buses instead of straight ahead at the front doors, they might have seen it. As it was, nobody saw the shadow that sprung up out of nothing. Nobody saw it take the shape of a twelve-year-old girl, and nobody saw it glow with light, and nobody saw the coppery-haired girl stumble up and out of it and onto the sidewalk.

Nobody, except a sixth-grade boy. He was standing on the sidewalk and had watched the whole thing with wide eyes. He watched the girl brush herself off, sigh with relief, and say, "Good shadow."

The shadow seemed pleased with itself, its light flickering a little before going out.

Well, thought Aria as the edges of the shadow reattached themselves to her heels. *That settles that.*

"Settles what?" asked the boy, and Aria looked up, realizing that she was visible again, *and* had spoken out loud.

"Can't fly," she said.

The boy's eyes widened a little more. "What are you?"

Aria sighed. Not *who*, which would have been easy to answer, but *what*. No one had asked Aria that, and she chewed her lip, and opened her mouth, and was about to answer when a bell rang in the distance. She cracked a grin.

"Late for class," she said, then waved good-bye and jogged toward the school.

On her way, she noticed that one of her laces — still pink — had come undone. She knelt to retie it, and while she was there, she decided to make them yellow instead. As her fingers redid the knot and then the bow, color slid out from her touch and along the shoestrings. She retied the laces on the other shoe, to make them even, and by the time she finished, both shoes were sporting laces the color of lemons. Aria smiled, and straightened, and looked up at the school.

GRAND HEIGHTS MIDDLE SCHOOL, read the marquee over the doors. This must be Gabby's school. Aria followed the wave of students inside, scanning the hall for signs of the other girl. She didn't see her. To be fair, it was a very large school, and there were a lot of kids. The hospital had been large, too, but Gabby stood out there, and here she'd blend right in.

Except, of course, for her blue smoke.

Not that Aria would be able to see it, with so many people — some of them tall! — in her way.

"There you are!"

Aria spun, but the girl who'd shouted those words wasn't talking to her.

"Move it, loser."

Aria frowned and turned, but the boy who'd said it was nudging someone else.

"I've missed you."

"Clear a path!"

"No food in the hall."

"Ugh."

Laughter. Slamming lockers. Scuffing shoes. A group of boys jostled for a soccer ball. A huddle of girls flipped

47

through the pages of a magazine. The whole school hummed with a kind of terrifying energy, and Aria hoped that wherever Gabby was, she was okay. Grand Heights Middle School wasn't just large, it was *loud*. A quiet person could drown in this much noise.

But Aria wouldn't let her.

Another bell rang, high and sharp over the sounds of the students, and the hall began to empty. Aria shifted her weight from foot to foot. Everyone was going to class, and she knew she couldn't just keep wandering around, looking for Gabby. Somebody — a teacher — would catch her and ask questions, as long as she was visible.

Still shaken from her last vanishing act and the fall, Aria took a deep breath and braced herself for the strange, vaguely uncomfortable feeling of disappearing.

But nothing happened.

Aria stared down at her hand and the blue charm bracelet around her wrist, both still visible. She thought again that she should probably be invisible. Again, she wasn't.

Aria didn't know if she was drained from the morning's mishap, or if the magic didn't come because she didn't *need* it, or if deep down, she didn't *want* to be invisible. Whatever the reason, it looked like Aria was going to be playing the role of student, and that meant she'd need to blend in. She looked around at the other kids in the hall. There didn't seem to be a uniform, or any standard outfit — most of them wore jeans and T-shirts — so she could keep her blue leggings and her white pocket skirt, but she needed a backpack.

A moment later she felt the strap in her hand and Aria was pleased to discover how bright the backpack was, a kind of iridescent fabric that changed colors in the light.

She caught her reflection in a glass case and marveled. She looked like a student!

The hall was almost empty, and Aria was about to pick a class at random when she saw something vanishing into a room ahead. Blue smoke.

Aria smiled and ran to catch up.

chapter 7

GABBY

"Hey, how was break?"

"Dang, you got tall."

"I love your hair."

"Still scrawny, Parker!"

"Where did you go this summer?"

"Where did the summer *go*?"

All around Gabby, kids were talking, but none of them were talking about her. Or Marco. None of them looked at her with worry. Because none of them looked at her at all.

Gabby quickly realized that the best thing about Grand Heights Middle School was also the scariest. No one knew who she was. As she made her way down the hall she told herself that's what she'd wanted. The chance to be somebody new. But she hadn't thought about the fact that until she became that somebody, she was *nobody*.

Marco could walk into a room and say hello, could start new relationships with one word. Gabby couldn't even will her feet forward. She *imagined* walking up to a group of girls at a locker and saying hi. But she couldn't.

The conversations happening all around her were like closed loops. She couldn't seem to find a way in. Everyone had these strings running between them, connecting their lives. And Gabby knew that all conversations involved questions. Such as:

What did you do this summer?

How would she even answer?

I just moved here.

Oh, really? they might say. *Where did you come from? Why did you move?*

And what would she say to that?

Lying would feel like a betrayal to Marco, but telling the truth would ruin everything. They'd stop seeing Gabby and start seeing some sick kid's sister instead. Maybe they'd retreat. Or maybe they'd look at her the way Alice and Beth had started to. Maybe they would hang out with her out of pity.

Gabby couldn't stand the thought of *that*, and she was saved from the anguish by the morning bell, which rang out overhead. The chattering students broke apart and hurried into classrooms. Gabby hoisted her bag onto her shoulder and followed them.

Her first class was English. The room was filling fast, and most of the groups from the hall had simply reformed around the desks. Gabby sighed, slid into an empty chair, and put her head down a moment on the desk.

"Is this seat taken?" asked a familiar voice, and Gabby looked up to find Aria standing at the desk beside her, one sneaker resting on the chair, her laces sunshine yellow. Happiness rolled through Gabby. She didn't realize how badly she wanted to see someone she knew . . . or at least, someone who wasn't a total stranger.

"I didn't know you went to Grand Heights," Gabby said.

"Me either," said Aria cheerfully. "It's my first day. I mean, I guess it's everyone's first day, but it's my *first* first."

Gabby frowned. "You didn't go here last year?"

"Nope," said Aria. "I just moved to Grand Heights." She brightened. "Like you! We should stick together," she added.

Gabby smiled a little, caught up in the relief of not being alone. The teacher rapped on the board.

"Hello, class! My name is Mr. Robert." Gabby already knew this because his name was written in three different places in the classroom — on the door, on the board, on the desk — as if the teacher was afraid the students would forget.

"I know what you're all thinking," he continued. "No, I'm not one of those hip teachers who goes by his first name." Gabby doubted anyone was thinking that. "My first name is Bertrand," said Mr. Robert. "But don't call me that. . . ."

Mr. Robert passed a stack of papers down each of the rows as he talked, and the girl in front of Gabby — who was tall and blond, with a high-wattage smile — turned and handed her a page. The girl bobbed her head back and forth as Mr. Robert rambled on, mouthing along, and Gabby nearly giggled.

"Charlotte," warned Mr. Robert, and the blond girl winked at Gabby and then spun forward. "Now, on to roll call."

He went down the list, and Gabby tried to remember the names and the faces that went with them, but she quickly lost track. Was the boy with the short black hair Evan or Ethan? Was the girl with the red glasses and the ponytail Mandy or Morgan? Gabby stole a glance at Aria and was surprised to find her staring intently at the paper in Mr. Robert's hand with a small frown. He made it all the way down the list before he called her name.

"Here!" said Aria brightly.

"Aria, I'm afraid I only have your first name," said Mr. Robert, taking up a pen. "What's your last name?"

Aria's brow furrowed. "Oh, no," she said. "I'm pretty sure it's always been Aria."

The students around her began to laugh. Gabby smiled. Mr. Robert sighed.

"I mean your *last name*. As in, the one that comes *after* your first name."

Aria frowned, and began to fidget with the charm bracelet around her wrist. "Oh," she said, looking down at it. "Um . . . blue!"

"Blue?" said Mr. Robert, raising a brow. "Like the color?"

Aria nodded. "Exactly. Aria Blue."

Mr. Robert shrugged, wrote in the last name, and set the sheet aside.

"All right, class. Let's get started." He leaned back against his desk. "You might think this is just an English class, but it's not. It's an *expression* class. We're going to be learning to use our words to tell our own stories. To that end, I want you each to dedicate a notebook to this class. You'll be given journal assignments over the course of the year. Some days you'll take the journal home, and some days you'll leave it with me, so don't think this is going to be one of those projects you can skip out on. I'll be checking in. And I hope you'll all embrace it, because we're going to start today."

The class groaned. Gabby groaned with them.

"Everyone take out a notebook."

Gabby took out the journal covered with music notes.

"Now," instructed Mr. Robert. "Turn to the first page —" A hand shot up. "You cannot possibly have questions yet, Jordan." The hand came back down. "Your first writing assignment is as simple as it gets. An introduction. I want you to introduce yourself to me. To the reader. I know that a blank page can seem daunting . . ." he added, "but I think you'll find that once you make the first mark, the rest will follow."

He turned and rounded his desk and wrote on the board.

Introduction.

Fun facts.

How I spent my summer.

All around the room, pencils and pens began to scratch and glide across the paper, but Gabby's pen hovered over the blank page. She couldn't think of a way to introduce herself, not without introducing Marco, and she couldn't tell Mr. Robert about her brother. When her old teachers back home found out, life became *Oh, Gabby dear, if you need more time* . . . and *Oh, Gabby, I know it's been hard* . . . and *Oh, Gabby, if you can't focus* . . .

She knew they didn't mean to make her feel different, but they did, and if Mr. Robert found out, it would happen all over again.

To her surprise, Gabby wasn't the only one struggling. She stole a look at Aria's journal and saw that it was blank, too, except for *My name is Aria Blue and I*

Gabby wondered how someone like Aria could have trouble finding words. She seemed so . . . *interesting*. The kind of girl who'd have tons of things she'd want to write about. But staring at the girl's blank page, Gabby realized something: she knew absolutely nothing about Aria Blue.

When the bell rang, Gabby's notebook was still blank. The blond girl in front of her — Charlotte — had filled half a dozen pages, and the other students Gabby could see from her seat had all written at least a few pages.

"Your homework," announced Mr. Robert, "is to finish introducing yourself and to introduce your family. Be specific. Be observant. Life is a story, so tell it."

Gabby and Aria got to their feet with the rest of the room and went to leave with the rest of the room, but Mr. Robert stopped them.

"Miss Blue, Miss Torres," he said. "Unless you've developed a new way of writing that doesn't involve moving your pen, I'm guessing you did not participate in today's exercise." He held out his hand. "Your journals, please."

Gabby's heart pounded as she reluctantly offered her teacher the notebook. He flipped it open and clicked his tongue at the blank pages. Her gaze went to the linoleum floor.

"I didn't know how to start," she mumbled.

"Yes, well, starting is the hard part. Do *you* have an excuse for not working, Miss Blue?"

Aria shrugged. "I haven't lived enough to write about it."

Mr. Robert gave her a sad smile. "How very existential," he said. Gabby didn't know what that meant, but then again she didn't really understand half of what he said. "But I'm willing to bet you've got something to say." He handed the journals back. "I'll be collecting these tomorrow at the end of class, so I suggest you find *something* to write about."

Gabby's heart started to sink, but Aria flashed her a smile.

"Don't worry," she said. "We will."

chapter 8

ARIA

Aria carried her lunch tray to the register in the cafeteria. When the lady told her how much she owed, Aria hesitated. She'd never needed money, but money was a *thing* and she was pretty good at making things out of nothing. So she dug her hand into the pocket of her skirt, and willed the money to be there, and a second later produced a fistful of cash and coins. She handed it over to the lunch lady without counting, and the lunch lady marveled at the fact it was *exactly* the right amount of money — not a penny more, not a penny less.

"Smart pockets," explained Aria with a smile.

The noise in the cafeteria was deafening. Aria saw that Gabby had already gotten her food and was standing at the edge of the sea of tables. She was clutching her tray and looking terrified. The blue smoke swirled nervously around her shoulders.

Aria had to admit, the cafeteria *was* daunting. But Gabby didn't have to face it alone.

She bumped Gabby's elbow.

"Let's find a seat."

They snagged a small table in a corner of the room.

"Everything on your plate is red," observed Gabby.

Aria looked down at her plate. It was true. She'd grabbed an apple and some kind of pasta with sauce and a bowl of Jell-O (even though it scared her). She'd never eaten before. She knew she didn't strictly *need* to eat, but it looked enjoyable. Besides, she was a student now. Other students ate. But her tray was looking less and less appetizing.

"I thought it would be fun," she explained, "to pick by color." She poked the Jell-O with a fork. "Everything was so bright and pretty piece by piece, but all together it's kind of a mess." Aria thought about the way she felt seeing herself for the first time, the whole so much better than the parts. "I guess food doesn't really work like people."

Gabby looked at Aria like she'd said a strange thing but then smiled.

"So, Aria Blue," she said. "That's a really cool name."

Aria beamed. "Thanks!" She was pretty proud of it. She hadn't realized when she'd imagined her name on the roster that she'd need *two*. At first she'd been at a total loss, but then she'd seen the bracelet and thought *blue*. It was the color of the smoke that circled those marked for her. It was part of her identity, just like a name. "I really like yours, too," she told Gabby.

Gabby shrugged. "It's a family name. Gabrielle. It's my grandmother's name. And my aunt's. And, like, four other relatives. When that many people have something, it starts to feel a little less special."

"There may be other Gabrielles," said Aria, "but there's only one Gabby."

"Actually, I'm pretty sure there are other Gabbys, too," said Gabby.

Aria ran a hand through her hair and accidentally snagged her charm bracelet. "What I mean," she said, tugging it free, "is that there's only one *you*. Only one *me*. And we get to be whoever we want, and no one can be us like we can. Isn't that exciting?"

Gabby gave a half-smile. "You're really different."

"One of a kind," said Aria with a wink. "Sooo" — she poked at the Jell-O again — "is Grand Heights Middle School everything you wanted it to be?"

Gabby shrugged lightly, but Aria watched the smoke coil and twist around her.

"My mom wanted to homeschool me," said Gabby. "She thought it would be easier, and maybe it would have been, but I begged her not to." Gabby picked at her food. "It wouldn't be homeschooling. It would be *hospital*-schooling, and I thought, if I was trapped in that place all day, every day, I'd just . . . disappear. But I'm here, surrounded by all these new kids, and I *still* feel kind of invisible."

"I see you," said Aria. "But I know what you mean."

"You do?"

Aria gave a somber nod. "I've been invisible. It's awful." Gabby looked surprised. "I mean, not . . . literally . . . of course," amended Aria hastily.

"But you're so . . . bright," said Gabby.

Aria looked down at herself. "I guess so."

"I didn't mean it in a bad way," said Gabby. "Just that you stand out. . . . I wish I did."

Aria shrugged. "I wear these colors because they make me happy, not because they make me stand out. I don't really think wearing loud clothes is the only way to be loud. I mean, sure," she added, "if you go around wearing neon-pink pajamas, people are going to look at you, but that doesn't mean you're going to be *seen.*" Aria took a cautious bite of her apple. "I think there's a difference."

"Maybe," said Gabby. "I don't really *want* to be loud. I just don't want to be invisible." Gabby's eyes escaped to her tray.

Aria looked around. "Well, the cafeteria is full of people. Why don't we make friends with some of them?"

Gabby gave her a withering look. "It's not that easy."

"Why not?"

Gabby chewed her lip. "Because it's not. Not for me."

"It'll be fine, come on!" Aria sprung up from the table, but Gabby grabbed her arm.

"Please don't," said Gabby, shaking her head. "Please don't make a scene."

Aria didn't understand, but Gabby seemed genuinely worried, so she sat back down. What Gabby needed was a little confidence. A chance to stand out in her own way.

Aria watched as Gabby hurriedly finished eating and then pulled a printed flier out of her bag.

"What's that?" asked Aria, trying to read upside down.

"It's a club list. Didn't you get one with your class schedule?"

Aria shook her head. "They must have left mine out," she said, which wasn't strictly a lie. "What's it for?"

"Grand Heights Middle has a bunch of after-school clubs," said Gabby, "and you can pick one, and I was thinking that maybe . . ." She looked down at the list and shrugged. "I don't know . . . maybe it's lame but —"

"This is perfect!" said Aria brightly.

"It is?" asked Gabby, surprised.

Aria nodded, and plucked the list out of Gabby's hands. There were more than a dozen choices. Cheerleading. Painting. Pottery. Track. Dance. *Perfect*, she echoed to herself. Gabby could find her own way to stand out!

"Which one are you going to pick?" Aria asked, handing the sheet back.

Gabby shook her head. "I don't know. We have all week to try them out before we have to decide. Do you think you'll do one, too?"

Aria could hear the hope in her question.

"Yeah, sure!" said Aria. "Sounds like fun."

"Which one do you think you'll choose?"

Aria hesitated. She didn't want to sway Gabby. "Tell you what," she said. "I'm not picky. Whatever you choose, I'll go with you. For moral support."

Gabby's eyes widened. "You would do that?"

Aria beamed. The fluorescent cafeteria lights brightened a fraction overhead. "Yep. So what do you think?"

Gabby looked down at the sheet. "I used to run track. . . ."

"Do you like it?"

"I did," said Gabby. "I'm not sure anymore."

"Well," said Aria as the lunch bell rang, "only one way to find out."

chapter 9

GABBY

"I don't think this is such a good idea," said Gabby after school. A sick feeling was forming in her stomach.

"Nonsense," said Aria, guiding her down toward the track. "It's a gorgeous day," she added.

It was, but a strange tightness was working its way into Gabby's chest. It had started back in the cafeteria and followed her through the afternoon classes and past the last bell, worsening as she changed into gym clothes and made her way out the doors to the rubber ring that ran around the soccer field.

She tried to swallow her nerves as she and Aria reached the dozen or so students gathered at the edge of the track, standing around a coach with a clipboard.

"All right, guys!" boomed the coach, even though everyone was well within earshot. "Huddle up!"

A couple of thin, long-legged girls — *they look like deer*, thought Gabby, *born to lope* — chuckled. A boy sniffed his armpit. The coach passed the clipboard around and everyone signed their name and then started to stretch and warm up. Aria mimicked them, but it was obvious she had no idea what she was doing.

"Are you sure you're up for this?" asked Gabby. "Have you ever run before?"

Aria looked down at her laces, which were now teal — Gabby could have sworn they'd been yellow this morning — and then back up. "I'm a fan of new experiences."

"Now," said the coach, "a few things you should know . . ." He started rambling on about track rules — no pushing, no tripping, et cetera — and Gabby's gaze drifted past the track to another group of students huddled in the middle of the field. Eighth graders, by the looks of them, passing a soccer ball back and forth. The tightness in her chest got worse.

"Hey, you okay?" asked Aria, and Gabby dragged her attention back and nodded absently, automatically, even though she didn't feel very okay.

"Yeah, why?"

Aria chewed her lip. "Well, it's just, he blew his whistle,

and everyone else started running and we're still standing here."

Gabby whipped her head around to see that Aria was right. All the other students were jogging around the track, at least a quarter of a lap ahead.

"Anytime now . . ." shouted the coach. Gabby drew a deep breath and took off.

Gabby hadn't run in more than a year, but she was still good at it. And for a moment, as the rubber track fell away under her shoes, everything was fine. She remembered the thrill of pumping legs and pounding heart. She'd forgotten how good it felt.

And then she thought of being in the woods behind their old house, racing Marco up the hill, the moment when she passed him and looked back and knew that something was wrong. The thrill dissolved into panic, and Gabby staggered to a halt halfway around the track, unable to breathe.

"What's wrong?" asked Aria, catching up and coming to a stop beside her.

Gabby squeezed her eyes shut. *This* was wrong. This was all wrong without Marco. Running was something she did because of him. Something they were supposed to do together.

"I can't do this," gasped Gabby.

"Sure you can," said Aria.

"No, I mean, I can't do *this*. I can't do track. I don't want to."

Before Aria could say anything else, Gabby turned and hurried away. She cut across the field to the bleachers and sank down onto a low metal bench, her head in her hands.

A few seconds later, she felt Aria sit down beside her on the bleachers and then a hand come to rest on her shoulder. Gabby usually hated those small physical gestures — nurses and doctors used them all the time — but she didn't mind it from Aria. It was strangely calming.

"I started running because of Marco," Gabby whispered without looking up. "He wanted to get in shape for soccer, and I wanted to spend time with him. He's the one who taught me how to sprint. It's hard enough that I'm going to school and he's not. I can't do track without him. I can't take it away from him."

"You're not taking anything away, Gabby," said Aria gently.

"I'm sorry," said Gabby, shaking her head, "but this is his. It doesn't feel right without him. I need something else. Something that isn't so . . . full of memories."

She closed her eyes and took a few long, slow breaths, in through her nose and out through her mouth, the way the doctor had told Marco to breathe if he felt a wave of panic coming on.

"She okay?" Gabby heard a girl ask from the track.

"She will be," said Aria. When Gabby opened her eyes she saw the girl — one of the graceful runners — jogging away. Then Gabby looked over at Aria, who was holding the sheet with the electives on it and looking over the other options.

"We'll pick something else for tomorrow," Aria said cheerfully. "Something brand-new."

chapter 10

ARIA

"What about cheerleading?"

"No way."

"Debate?"

"Are you kidding?"

They were making their way to the hospital. Gabby kicked a pebble down the sidewalk while Aria crossed out after-school options with a blue pen.

"Foreign language?" she offered.

"Two languages is enough for me," said Gabby. "Do you speak any others?"

Aria shrugged. "I don't think so."

"My *abuela* only speaks Spanish," explained Gabby, "so Marco and I grew up speaking both that and English. My dad knew how to speak Spanish, but he didn't like my grandmother much, so he went out of his way to speak English when she was around."

Aria hesitated. Gabby hadn't mentioned him before. "Where's your dad now?" she asked carefully.

"Gone," said Gabby, kicking the pebble hard enough to send it skittering into the street. The blue smoke swirled and curled around her shoulders. "He left way before Marco got sick." She found another pebble and began to knock it along down the road. "Can I ask you something?"

"Sure," said Aria.

"Why didn't you write anything in your journal?"

Aria shrugged. "I didn't have anything to write about."

"What about your family?" asked Gabby.

Aria's steps slowed. "What about them?"

Gabby shrugged. "Couldn't you write about them? What are they like? What do they do? Do you have any brothers or sisters?"

Aria's heart twisted. She wasn't sad, not exactly — she knew she didn't need a family, knew that wasn't part of her purpose — but the questions left a strange emptiness in her chest. "It's complicated," she said at last. It wasn't a lie.

"I'm sorry," said Gabby. "I didn't mean to be nosy. I shouldn't have —"

"It's no problem," said Aria with a smile. "It's just . . . ooooooooh!"

She caught sight of a shop window and veered off the sidewalk and up to the glass. Inside was a shelf filled with brightly frosted cupcakes.

"So many colors," whispered Aria, peering in through the glass.

Gabby laughed. "It's tinted frosting," she explained. "Food coloring —"

But Aria had already gone in. The whole shop smelled sweet like sugar, and when she breathed in, she could taste it on her tongue. She spent several minutes wavering between a chocolate cupcake with pink icing and a vanilla cupcake with blue icing and a swirl cupcake with purple icing and ended up asking for half a dozen, two of each, so she and Gabby could both try all three.

They sat on a bench outside with the open box. Aria couldn't believe the cupcakes tasted even better than they smelled! She tried to pick her favorite and couldn't.

"Can I take one of these to Marco?" asked Gabby before biting into the swirl cupcake with purple icing.

"Of course," said Aria, who was now cutting two cupcakes apart and putting them back together in new combinations.

Gabby carefully nestled a vanilla cupcake with blue frosting into the container to keep it safe.

"Does Marco like cupcakes?" asked Aria.

"He likes anything that's not hospital food," said Gabby. "And I think it might cheer him up."

"You're a really, really good sister, Gabby," said Aria, taking a big bite of cupcake. Gabby blushed.

Cupcakes devoured, the girls continued on toward the hospital. As it came into view up ahead, Aria yawned.

"What was that?" she asked, surprised.

"Sugar crash," said Gabby, suppressing a yawn herself. "It happens when you eat a lot of sugar and get really hyper and then you get really tired. Maybe you shouldn't have tried *all* the cupcakes."

Aria yawned again. "Tired?"

"Yeah. Tired. You know. The feeling you get when you need to sleep."

Aria stared at Gabby. "But I don't . . ." She trailed off with a frown, then said, "I don't normally get tired."

"Well, you don't normally eat a pound of sugar, do you?"

"No," she admitted, yawning a third time as they crossed the parking lot.

"Do you have to volunteer today?" asked Gabby. Aria shook her head. "Then why did you come with me?"

Aria shrugged. "I just thought I'd keep you company."

Gabby started to smile. And then they reached the gray hospital steps, and her smile faded. Gabby's shoes came to a stop, her fingers tightening on the cupcake box as she stared up at the revolving doors. Aria watched the blue smoke, which had calmed a little, swirl into motion again, engulfing her. But before Aria could ask Gabby a question, the other girl took a deep breath.

"Let's go," she said, and started up the steps.

chapter 11

GABBY

Gabby cradled the cupcake box as she and Aria wove through the halls toward Marco's room. She knew he would be in a bad mood from missing school, so the cupcake seemed like the least she could do.

A tiny bit of blue sky, she thought, holding the box close.

When they got to his room, Gabby peered in through the window and let out a small sigh of relief when she saw that he was alone. It was easier that way. Marco liked to pretend things were normal almost as much as she did, and sometimes, if they were careful, they could get through a whole conversation without mentioning his condition or the hospital. They could carve those pieces out and focus on the other parts, ignoring the holes. When Gabby's mom was there, the holes were all she saw.

"Hey, Gabs," said Marco, looking up from his schoolwork as she and Aria came in. He gestured to the textbooks scattered on the bed. "I hope your first day was way more fun than mine."

"I survived," said Gabby, looking around. "No Henry?"

"He came by earlier," said Marco. And then his eyes went past her, to Aria. "You have a shadow."

"Marco, this is Aria," said Gabby. "Aria, Marco." She felt herself smile when she introduced them and realized she was proud to have gone to a new school and returned with a new . . . friend? Yes. Aria could definitely be considered a friend. "We go to Grand Heights together, and Aria also volunteers here," Gabby added.

"Aren't you kind of young?" Marco asked Aria.

"Do you have to be a certain age to help people?" asked Aria, sounding genuinely curious.

The edge of Marco's mouth went up. "No, I suppose not."

"We brought you a treat," said Gabby. "Better eat it before Mom shows up."

Gabby handed him the cupcake, and Marco nearly wept as he pulled it out of the box and dug in. He took only a couple of bites of the cupcake before he had to stop — these days his stomach couldn't keep up with his eyes — but he cradled it in his lap as if it really were a piece of blue sky, of freedom.

And then Gabby's mom came in.

The first words out of her mouth were, "Marco, what on earth are you eating?"

She swiped the cupcake out of his hands and deposited it on the side table, then produced a napkin and began wiping the frosting from his fingers.

Marco rolled his eyes. "If anything kills me," he said, pulling away, "it won't be a cupcake."

"Marco!" Gabby's mom scolded, appalled. He slumped back against his pillow as tears brimmed in Mrs. Torres's eyes.

Gabby sighed and said, "It was my fault."

Her mom turned and blinked, seeming to notice her for the first time.

"Gabrielle," she scorned, "you should know better."

"I know," said Gabby. "It's just, we stopped on the way back from *school*," she added, giving her mom a weighted look, "and I thought it would be a nice treat."

Mrs. Torres softened, then reached out and smoothed Gabby's hair. "Well, that was very sweet of you. And yes, school!" She perched on the nearest chair and took Gabby's hand. "How was it? Were your classes all right? Did you have what you needed?"

Gabby felt a hand at her shoulder as Aria whispered, "I'll be right back," and then both the hand and the voice slipped away. Gabby nodded absently, not wanting to lose her mom's attention.

"Go on. I want to hear all about it."

Her mom *said* that, and Gabby wanted to think she meant it, but she'd barely opened her mouth when a knock came at the door and a nurse came in, saying something about paperwork. Mrs. Torres's hand slid from Gabby's as she straightened and nodded and said *of course*, and followed the woman out.

Gabby stood there a moment, staring at the door, a tangle of emotions wrapping around her like smoke, thick and suffocating. And then a voice reached her through the cloud.

"Hey, Gabs," said Marco gently. "Forget her. Tell me. And remember I'm trying to live through you over here, so make it good."

Gabby hesitated, then nodded, and slid into the chair beside his bed.

"Now," said Marco, lifting the cupcake from the table and taking another, much smaller bite, "start at the beginning."

Gabby told Marco almost everything: from how left out she felt on the school bus to the journal assignment in

English to how she and Aria sat together at lunch. She didn't tell him about trying to run track and the fact that she couldn't bring herself to do it without him. It would only make him upset.

"Where did your friend run off to?" asked Marco when Gabby was finished.

She looked around the room, as if Aria might simply be hiding in a corner. "I don't know," she said, trying to hide her disappointment. "She probably went home."

"Speaking of, you should go, too," said Marco. Gabby frowned at the thought of the empty apartment but didn't complain, only dragged herself to her feet.

"Hey, Gabs," Marco added. "Thanks for the cupcake. It tasted like —"

"A piece of sky?" asked Gabby hopefully.

Marco smiled. He knew what she meant. "I'm not sure sky has that much sugar or artificial coloring, but yeah. It tasted like normal, and that's exactly what I needed today."

Gabby smiled back. "That's what I'm here for."

"I hope you don't feel like that," he said. "Some days I don't feel like I'm more than this — this sickness — but you are, okay? Don't be this place. Don't be . . ." He trailed off and then picked back up. "Just be you."

Gabby wondered who that was but didn't say that, only nodded.

"Night, Marco."

"Night, Gabs."

The orange cat was back on the apartment steps, catching moths. Gabby knelt and scratched behind its ears, wishing she could coax it to follow her up into the empty apartment, for company. Marco wasn't allergic, but when he got sick, Mom decided all four-legged creatures were germy carriers of evil.

Gabby went upstairs. She stomped on the floor and said hello to the ghosts and hummed while she made herself dinner. Then she turned on the radio and sank down onto her bed to do homework. It was a nice evening, and she left the window open, relishing the fresh air — not fresh like the woods behind their old house, but miles better than the hospital — while she worked.

Most of the assignments were easy enough, but when she got to English, she found herself staring down at the still-blank journal.

I'll be collecting these tomorrow at the end of class, Mr. Robert had said. *So I suggest you find something to write about.*

Gabby tapped her pencil against the page.

My name is Gabrielle Torres, she wrote.

I am twelve years old, and I don't know who I am. I know who I was when I was eleven, before my brother got sick, but somewhere between then and now I've lost it. Myself, I mean. I don't know how to find it again. I thought a self was something you always had, something that grew up with you. Something you couldn't lose. I thought you only got one self, but if that's the case, then what happens if you lose it? Do you try to find it, or replace it? I want to go back to being the person I was before, but it doesn't work that way. Before-Gabby doesn't exist anymore. And now? Now I don't know who I am.

That's what she *wanted* to write.

That's what she *should* have written.

But she couldn't do it.

Instead, she wrote a lie. It started as a small one — *My family just moved here so my mom could start a new job* — and then got it bigger — *My brother, Marco, is in tenth grade over at Grand Heights High* — and bigger — *He's going to try out for soccer soon* — spiraling away before Gabby could stop it. She wrote a paragraph, and then a page, and then two, all of it what she wanted to be true. A life where Marco had never gotten sick. A life where everyone was happy and healthy and Gabby didn't feel invisible.

And Gabby knew she should stop, knew this was wrong, but she liked the girl on the page more than she liked the one writing on it, and she wanted it to be real, even if it only felt real for a few moments.

So she kept writing.

chapter 12

ARIA

One minute Aria was sitting on the couch in the common room, and the next a hand was shaking her awake. For a dazed second, she had no idea where she was, and then she blinked and remembered. She'd been wandering through the hospital, trying to shake off the "sugar crash" and give Gabby some space.

She wanted to be there for her, of course, but she couldn't *always* be there. And it wouldn't do Gabby any good if she learned how to be herself only when Aria was with her.

Aria had made her way to the common room, hoping to see Henry and find out more about his purple-black smoke. Only he hadn't been there, and she couldn't stop yawning, so she'd decided to sit down and then . . . had she fallen *asleep?*

"Young lady," said the nurse, whose hand was still on her shoulder. "Visiting hours are over. It's time to go home."

Home? Aria nodded absently and looked around the common room, still groggy. Beyond the window, the sun was going down.

"Do you have family here?" pressed the nurse. "Is someone coming to pick you up?"

Gabby. Where was she?

"I live close by," said Aria, getting up.

She regretted the cupcakes as she trudged back through the hospital to Marco's room. When she got there, she saw Marco sitting up in bed, writing in a journal, but no Gabby. She double-regretted the cupcakes as she made her way downstairs and out the revolving doors onto the ugly gray steps of the hospital. And then she realized that she couldn't remember the way to Gabby's house.

The sinking sun and the glow of the hospital cast her shadow like a door on the concrete. Aria tapped her shoe, and the shadow fidgeted.

"I need to find Gabby," she told the shadow. "Take me home," she said, and then frowned and corrected herself. "I mean, take me to *Gabby's* home."

The shadow obligingly filled with light, and Aria said thank you and stepped through. An instant later she found herself stepping out of the glowing pool and onto the sidewalk in front of Gabby's building. The light went off inside the shadow, and Aria took a small step forward, nestling her shoes in the right place just as Gabby herself came through the front doors, a bag of trash in hand.

"Aria?" she asked, surprised. "Where did you come from?"

"The hospital," said Aria, grateful Gabby hadn't walked out a second sooner.

Gabby dropped the bag she was holding in the garbage bin. "What are you doing here?"

"I live nearby," said Aria. "And I thought I'd come and say hi. So . . . hi."

"Hi," said Gabby. A moment of silence fell between them. Aria waited. Gabby fidgeted. Finally she said, "You want to come upstairs?"

Aria smiled. "I'd love to."

She hopped up the steps but hesitated at the entrance. What if she still couldn't go in? But then Gabby held the door open for her and said, "You coming?" and Aria's shoe crossed the threshold without any resistance. She smiled and followed Gabby inside.

"Here we are," said Gabby when they reached her apartment.

Aria looked around. She'd never been in a home before, but she'd imagined it would feel . . . homier.

Gabby kicked off her shoes by the door, and Aria did the

same. She started to follow Gabby toward her room when she noticed a photo in the hall and stopped. It was the only decor in the hallway, and it had obviously been taken before Marco got sick. Gabby and Marco and their mom were all sitting around a table in a big backyard, wooded hills behind them. The photo wasn't faded, but there was something about it that made them seem far away. Gabby's mom was in the middle, her arms around her children, and they were all smiling.

"It's weird, right?" said Gabby, coming up beside her. "How different we look." She reached out and touched her fingertips to the glass. "We were a team until . . ." Her words fell away, and so did her fingers. "My room's this way."

Aria thought Gabby's room was nice — she didn't have any others to compare it to — but nothing about it really screamed *Gabby*. Then again, nothing about Gabby screamed *Gabby* yet. That was the problem. Aria thought about turning one of the walls a color — they were all a soft white — but she didn't know which color to make it, and besides, that might be hard to explain, so she held off.

Gabby flopped down on her bed. "Make yourself comfortable."

Aria wandered around the room, taking in the details. Gabby's closet door was open, and Aria could see dozens of outfits inside. Shirts and pants and skirts and shoes. Aria looked down at her own ensemble. It had never occurred to her to change. Aria made a mental note to do so at some point. She turned back toward the room. There was a radio on the table by Gabby's bed, and Aria crossed to it, mesmerized, and began pressing buttons, searching through stations.

"So you came just to say hi?" asked Gabby.

"I didn't want you to think I'd bailed on you," said Aria. "I fell asleep at the hospital."

Songs poured and crashed and seeped and sprang out of the radio as Aria clicked through.

"Can I ask you something?" said Gabby, getting suddenly quieter. "Why are you hanging out with me?"

Aria looked up from the radio, surprised. Gabby's smoke was swirling around her again, and Aria could practically hear the doubt spilling out of Gabby's head before she spoke.

"Is it because of my brother?" Gabby asked quickly.

Aria shook her head. "No. It doesn't have anything to do with Marco."

"Is it because you feel sorry for me?"

"I don't."

"Then why?" pressed Gabby.

Aria chewed her lip. "Because I want to help."

"So you *do* feel sorry for me."

"No," said Aria. "But I can tell you're going through a hard time, and I'm hanging out with you because I *want* to. Because I think you're really cool, even if you can't see it."

Gabby blushed, her eyes going to her bedspread. She mumbled something that sounded like, "No, I'm not."

"You are, too. The thing is," said Aria, searching for the words, "I have this . . . this superpower."

The corner of Gabby's mouth twitched. "No, you don't."

"I do!" said Aria cheerfully. "When I look at someone, I can see the way they are *and* the way they're going to be." It wasn't a lie, thought Aria. Not really. After all, she could see Gabby's smoke, and she knew she'd be better, happier, brighter, once the smoke was gone.

"And when you look at me?" asked Gabby.

"I see someone who's going to be *amazing*."

Gabby smiled, and the smoke around her wavered ever so slightly. "You really think so?"

"Yeah," said Aria. "I do."

Aria landed on a pop station, filling the room with cheerful music. She fell into a cushy chair in the corner and pulled out her homework. It seemed silly to do it, but as long as Aria was helping Gabby, she figured she *was* a student. For a second she wondered what would happen when it was over and time for her to go, but she pushed the thought away.

Gabby started humming along to the song on the radio. Aria didn't know the words, but she tried to sing along. She wasn't much good at it, but it didn't stop her from trying, and the two ended up giggling more than once when Aria managed to both be totally off-key and replace all the words with nonsense ones at the same time.

A couple hours later, Aria was in the middle of a particularly horrible sing-a-long when Gabby's phone rang. Gabby's smoke coiled around her, tensing, as she answered.

"Mom? Is everything okay?" The voice on the other end said something, and Gabby's shoulders relaxed visibly and then slumped. She mumbled something in Spanish and hung up.

"Everything all right?" asked Aria.

Gabby nodded. "She's going to stay awhile longer. Told me to go to bed." She yawned and looked at the clock. Aria could tell that it was time for her to leave.

"I better get going," she said.

"Do you need to call someone to come get you?"

"No," said Aria. "I don't live that far away."

Gabby looked out the window at the dark. "Do you want me to walk you home?"

Aria shook her head. "No," she said with a smile. "I'll let myself out."

"Hey," said Gabby when Aria had reached the bedroom door. "Thanks."

"For what?" asked Aria.

"For sticking with me."

Aria beamed. "I'll see you at school tomorrow," she said before slipping into the hall. She got to the front door and saw her shoes sitting in the foyer. Then she hesitated. Did she *have* to go? Would Gabby's mom come home? Would Gabby be all alone? It didn't seem right to leave Gabby by herself, not if she didn't have to, and even if Gabby couldn't see her, maybe she would feel less alone if Aria were there.

Aria made her decision. She slid into her shoes and considered her teal laces for a moment before willing them, along with the rest of her, to disappear.

"You pick," said Gabby at lunch the next day.

Aria was looking over the club list again. That morning, she'd managed to duck out of the apartment while Gabby was in the shower and met her on the front steps of the apartment building so they could ride the bus together. She'd even summoned up some new clothes and was now sporting a pair of jeans and a striped T-shirt.

The girls were at their table in the cafeteria, and Aria was determined to find Gabby the right after-school activity.

"I'm not picking," said Aria, "it has to be *your* choice."

"Why?" pressed Gabby. "It's your club time, too. You have just as much right to pick."

"You're only saying that," said Aria, poking the food on her tray (it was all orange), "because you don't want to choose."

Gabby sighed. "How am I supposed to?" she asked. "If the whole idea is to try something new, then I have to choose something I don't know if I'll like. It would be easier to just pick at random."

Aria brightened. "Okay! We'll do that."

"Wait, no," said Gabby, "I don't actually —"

Aria held up her hand. "This is a good idea," she said. She grabbed a pencil from her backpack, and she quickly counted the number of remaining options: eleven. She then numbered the activities out of order.

"Pick a number," Aria told Gabby, "one to eleven."

"But there are things on there that —"

"It's only Tuesday," said Aria, "and you said we have all week. If we don't like the club today, we'll pick a new one tomorrow. It'll be fun."

Gabby took a deep breath. "Okay. Seven."

Aria turned the paper around to show her what she'd chosen. *Dance*.

"Dance?" asked Gabby nervously. "But I don't know how."

"Perfect!" said Aria. "Neither do I!"

Dance did not go well.

Aria really liked it, but Gabby hated the mirrors in the studio. Every time she began to relax, even a little, she'd catch sight of her reflection and get self-conscious all over again.

The next day, they tried yearbook (option eight), which was a total bust because Aria wasn't very good with computers, having never seen one, and Gabby didn't know anything about the school or its students.

Thursday afternoon, they found themselves in painting (option two), and things weren't going much better. Aria was getting nervous because Gabby still hadn't found something that was *hers*, and they were running out of options, and out of time.

Aria sat at her easel and swirled the pigments on her palette. She liked the *idea* of painting but was frustrated by the fact that mixing two, three — even four — awesome colors didn't always result in a *more awesome* color. In fact, most of the time it just resulted in brown. She frowned down at the mess on her tray while one easel over Gabby seemed to be struggling with her own paints.

"Find form," the teacher told Aria when she saw the abstract swirls on the paper.

"Let go," the teacher told Gabby when she saw the rigid shapes on hers. Gabby's smoke rippled with frustration.

This *definitely* wasn't the right club, and Aria was almost relieved when Gabby turned toward her too fast and accidentally painted a streak of red across the yellow sundress Aria was wearing.

"I'm so sorry!" said Gabby, scrambling for paper towels, but Aria only smiled and waved her way.

"It's fine, don't worry," she said. "It'll come out."

Before Gabby could say anything else, Aria ducked out of the studio and ran her hand over the stain, the color vanishing with her touch, leaving the dress beneath spotless. Aria sighed and leaned back against the wall. If only fixing Gabby's problems were that easy.

One day left, she thought, pulling the list of options from her dress pocket. There had to be something here.

And then, just as she was about to head back into the art room, Aria heard the singing. It was soft and far away, and she followed it through the halls until she found a door covered in music notes, just like Gabby's journal. Aria pressed her ear to the door, listened, and smiled. A bunch of different voices were singing together inside the room. It was beautiful. She'd liked the music pouring out of Gabby's radio, but this was better.

Gabby could do this, thought Aria, pulling back.

Gabby would be *so good* at this.

Aria had heard Gabby humming when she walked and when she did homework and when she showered. She sounded great, but she did it only when she thought she was alone. And that was Gabby's problem, wasn't it?

But this. This could be her solution.

Aria hurried back to class, bouncing with excitement because she finally knew how to help Gabby find her voice.

chapter 13

GABBY

The next day at lunch, Gabby picked number six.

"Let's see. . . ." said Aria, squinting at the list. "That's choir!"

Gabby frowned. "I thought choir was number three."

Aria waved her hand. "No, it was totally number six."

"I don't know about this," said Gabby when they reached the music room. When she first saw the music notes covering the door, her spirits began to rise. But her excitement quickly gave way to nerves as she heard the students laughing and chatting on the other side of the door.

"Come on, Gabby," said Aria, rocking from heel to toe. "It'll be fun. And besides, you have a great voice. You're always humming."

"That's *humming*, Aria. This is *singing*. In front of people. There's a big difference."

The difference was that humming made her feel calm. The thought of singing in front of people made her feel sick.

"It's singing *with* people," said Aria. "And really singing is just humming with more words."

Gabby hesitated. But it was Friday, which meant it was the last day to test out activities, and she was running out of chances. She took the smallest possible step toward the door and stopped. "Are you sure about this?" she asked. "Don't take this the wrong way, but singing isn't exactly *your* greatest strength."

"Lucky for you, I don't mind looking silly," said Aria.

Gabby's shoulders loosened as she laughed, and before she could come up with another protest, Aria put her hands on her back and pushed her into the room.

It was larger than Gabby expected, one wall holding instruments and the other made up into a small mock stage. A dozen kids sat on foldout chairs in a messy circle.

A pair of twin girls was trying to land candy in each other's mouths. Gabby recognized them from math class, and knew their names were Emmie and Ellie but couldn't remember who was who.

A boy she didn't know was lying on the floor with his head on his backpack, wearing massive headphones. Another boy was rapping to a group of three girls huddled in a circle, all clearly pretending to ignore him. Gabby remembered seeing the trio in the hall the first day, elbows linked even then in a way that very clearly said *This group is closed.*

The trio turned as a group, sizing up Gabby and Aria as they came in. Gabby could feel herself starting to shrink when someone laughed loudly. Gabby looked over to see the tall blond girl from English class. Charlotte. They'd said only a handful of words to each other all week, but she'd always seemed friendly. Today she was chatting with a boy nearly a foot shorter than Gabby, and he was passing a soccer ball from hand to hand as they talked.

When Charlotte caught sight of Gabby, she waved but didn't interrupt the boy, who was gesturing enthusiastically, clearly telling a story.

Just then the door swung open again and a woman came in on a wave of sound. Her bracelets chimed and her earrings tinkled and her skirts *shhhhshhh*ed and her voice when she spoke had a musical rhythm.

"Afternoon, my dears," she said. "I'm Ms. Riley. Gather 'round." The room filled with the sound of scraping chairs as the kids made a tighter, cleaner circle, and Gabby and Aria joined the group.

"We have a few new songbirds today, I see," said Ms. Riley, nodding at Gabby, Aria, and the boy who'd been lying on the floor and was now sitting in a chair, headphones hanging around his neck. "Whatever brings you here, welcome. I hope I'm not a last resort." Ms. Riley clapped her hands. "Now, let's loosen up those voices and those nerves and play a singing game."

Gabby fidgeted nervously in her seat, but Aria gave her an encouraging smile. Ms. Riley passed out a few pages of songs and explained the rules. The whole group would sing the first stanza and the chorus, and then they'd go around the circle, each singing a line, then everyone would do the chorus, and so on.

"A vocal hot potato!" Ms. Riley explained excitedly, and Gabby realized she liked this teacher. "Charlotte," Ms. Riley said. "We'll start with you."

"You want me on piano?" asked the short boy with the soccer ball.

"Not right now, Sam," said Ms. Riley. "Voices only at the moment. Ready? Let's go."

Charlotte cleared her throat, and began to sing. Her voice was beautiful and clear as a bell, and Gabby started to think she'd made a horrible mistake, letting Aria drag her here. Her chest tightened at the thought of singing after Charlotte. But then the song passed to Sam. Sam was nowhere near as good, but he fumbled cheerfully through the line. He reminded Gabby of Aria, the way he didn't get embarrassed or shy. The boy with the headphones came next, and he was good — *very* good — and then it was Aria's turn and she was just as delightfully bad as Gabby remembered. Gabby bit back a giggle as Aria missed the notes.

And then it was *her* turn.

For a fraction of a second, Gabby froze. The song hung in the air, the sound dying off. Panic tightened around her chest.

But then she shook it free. What was she afraid of? Messing up? Sam had. Sounding off-key? Aria had. It wasn't such a big deal.

Gabby drew in a breath and began to sing. She was a beat or two late, but she picked up the line and didn't drop it. A rush of relief flooded her face as she got the last note out and passed the song along.

Charlotte winked at her across the circle. Gabby smiled, and when the group picked up the chorus, she was there, singing as loudly as the rest, and when the song came back to her, she didn't fumble it at all.

By the end of the third song, Gabby had forgotten her fears and was actually starting to *enjoy* herself. She didn't have to think, didn't have to find words. She could just focus on the music and the lyrics. They swept her up, carried her

along, and the current was enough that when she was singing, she nearly forgot about . . . everything. And then the
song trailed away, and Gabby found herself back in reality.

"Very good, very good," chimed Ms. Riley as everyone
gathered up their bags. "Gabrielle, Aria, Brendan," she said,
offering them each a piece of paper. "You'll need to get this
signed if you're going to stay." Her eyes found Gabby's. "And
I really hope you do."

It was a permission slip. Gabby had collected them from
track, dance, yearbook, painting, and now choir.

"Just bring the slip back signed on Monday," said Ms.
Riley, "and you're in the club."

Gabby folded the paper and tucked it into her bag and
was halfway to the door with Aria when someone called her
name. She turned to find Charlotte and the boy with the
soccer ball, Sam.

"How long have you been singing?" Charlotte asked
Gabby.

Gabby shrugged. "I've never really done it before."

"Seriously?" said Sam.

"You're really good!" said Charlotte.

Gabby blushed.

"You're going to join the club, right?" pressed Charlotte.

Gabby shrugged. She hated herself for shrugging, but she didn't know what else to do. It was one thing, sitting in a circle, but it was another getting up onstage and singing in front of people.

"You should," said Sam. "It'll be fun."

"Yeah," added Charlotte. "And you're a natural. You'll fit in perfectly."

By the time Gabby caught up with Aria in the hall, she could feel herself beaming.

"Well?" asked Aria, bouncing on her toes, clearly pleased with herself.

"Much better than painting," said Gabby.

Aria nodded. "And way less messy."

chapter 14

ARIA

Aria's heart thudded happily. She'd done it. She'd found something for Gabby.

When Gabby had started singing in the circle, her smoke began to shift, to change. Aria had watched it ripple and — for a little while — thin. The smoke had come back, of course, by the time they reached the hospital. But it was a sign, a step — even a small one.

"What are you smiling about?" asked Gabby as they ambled down the sidewalk.

"Nothing," said Aria. "Just thinking."

They walked in an easy silence up the hospital steps. They'd fallen into a routine, heading there together each day after school. Later on, Aria would follow Gabby home — now that she'd been invited in, she could come and go — and make sure she was okay alone. Gabby's mom came home most nights, but Gabby was usually asleep, and even when she wasn't, Mrs. Torres's being there didn't make the house much warmer. Gabby and her mom just sat at the table, eating dinner while the TV rambled in the background.

At the hospital, Aria and Gabby found Marco flipping through channels on a TV mounted to his wall.

"Thank god you're here," he muttered when he saw them. "Mom's at her worst. I sent her on some errand for an obscure caffeine-free healthy soda just to get a few moments of peace."

Gabby frowned. "Why is she hovering? Did something happen?"

He shook his head and tossed the remote onto the bed. "I had *one* small coughing fit. It wasn't even that bad, but I got dizzy and she freaked out."

"Are you okay now?"

"Of course I'm okay." He rubbed his eyes. "I was okay *then*, too. But I'm losing it, Gabs. They better clear me for surgery soon 'cause I can't keep doing this. I can't stay in here. I can't . . ."

His breathing started to tighten, and Marco closed his eyes and rested his head on his knees. Gabby hurried forward and began rubbing circles on his back and whispering in Spanish. Aria hesitated by the door, watching Gabby's smoke engulf them both. Aria didn't know what to do. She wished that she could make Marco better, but her powers didn't work that way.

Gabby picked up the remote. "Let's find something good," she said, flipping through channels. It didn't seem to help. "Do you want me to go get Henry?" she finally asked.

Marco nodded silently.

"I'll go find him," offered Aria.

Gabby gave her a look that was equal parts surprise and relief. "You sure?"

Aria nodded. "He's in 308," said Gabby, adding a small, "Thank you."

Aria wove through the halls to the other side of the floor, stopping outside room 308. When she peered in through the glass insert, she saw the boy sitting in bed, pale as the sheets, his purple-black smoke still hanging cloudlike around his shoulders. Why hadn't anyone like Aria come to help him yet?

A book sat open in his lap, but he was staring past it into space. And then, as if he could sense Aria there, he turned his head and saw her. He gave a small wave.

Aria pushed open the door and stepped inside.

"Hi, Henry," she said.

"Do I know you?" he asked.

She shook her head. "I'm Aria," she said.

"You're Gabby's friend," said Henry. Aria's heart fluttered at the word. *Friend*. She liked the idea of being a *friend* almost as much as she liked being an *Aria*. "Marco told me about you," he explained.

"What did he say?" asked Aria.

"That you were strange," said Henry. A shadow of a smile touched his mouth. "And that you were cool." He tried to hold on to the smile, but underneath it he looked so *sad*. Aria's eyes kept going back to the dark smoke that hung around him like a fog.

"Are you okay?" she asked.

Henry's watery blue eyes took her in. "That's a silly thing to ask someone in a hospital."

Aria felt herself blush. "I'm sorry. I didn't mean big okay," she said, spreading her arms. "I just meant little okay." She brought her hands together, leaving only a few inches between them.

"Just tired," he said, adding, "My parents were here. I'm always tired after they visit." The second part he'd said so softly Aria had barely heard.

"Why's that?" she asked.

Henry opened his mouth like he wanted to say something but thought better of it. "I don't know," he said, picking up his book and pretending to read. She could tell he was pretending because his eyes never moved from the middle of the page. When Aria didn't leave, Henry looked up from his pretend-reading and said, "So what brings you to my rather gloomy quarters?"

Aria chewed her lip. "I came to see if you want to watch TV with Gabby and Marco."

Henry started to shake his head. But Aria knew that Gabby's brother needed him and she could tell that Henry needed to get out of this room, so she said, "Marco's not doing great. I think he'd really like it if you came."

At that, Henry's face changed again. He didn't ask what was wrong, only straightened and nodded.

"Well, then," he said, mustering a smile. "I'll be his knight in shining armor." He pointed to the wheelchair. "Grab my steed."

A nurse stopped them in the hall, and after a few minutes of bickering with Henry over his outing, insisted on accompanying them to Marco's room. Henry sighed and let the nurse push him the rest of the way. Marco looked up when they came in, his eyes hanging on Henry's for a moment.

Henry didn't say *"What's wrong?"* or *"Where does it hurt?"* or *"Are you okay?"* All he said was, "You good, Torres?"

Marco nodded. "Yeah."

"Good," said Henry. And that was that. And looking at them, at the defiance in Henry's eyes when he asked the question and the set of Marco's jaw when he answered, Aria understood why they didn't ask each other silly questions. Everyone else treated them like patients. They treated each other like people. Like friends.

Friends listened when you needed to talk and they didn't make you talk when you didn't want to and they knew how to help you without making you feel like you needed help.

You're Gabby's friend, Henry had said.

Aria smiled. Gabby was sitting next to Marco's bed, and Marco was already chatting with Henry and acting like himself again. Gabby met Aria's eyes and mouthed *thank you*.

"Only thirty minutes," insisted the nurse, still gripping Henry's chair. He waved her tiredly away.

Then he wheeled himself over to Marco's bed and kicked his legs up onto the sheets.

"No time to waste, Torres," he said. "What are we watching?"

chapter 15

GABBY

Marco made the soccer team this week, Gabby wrote in her journal on Sunday. *No one's surprised,* she added. *He's always been the best.*

She paused and reread the lines. Then she added a few about Henry.

In journal-world, Henry lived in the same building as Marco and Gabby, and that's how they first met over the summer.

Henry never seems very happy, wrote Gabby, *but he's good at making other people happy, especially Marco.*

And then, without thinking, Gabby wrote: *I really hope he gets better.*

Gabby froze. The line sat there in the middle of the page, a glaring piece of truth in a book filling up with lies, and suddenly Gabby felt horrible. Horrible for messing up the lie, and horrible for wanting to make the truth go away in the first place.

Gabby began to scribble out the line, and pressed down so hard she tore the paper. She let out an exasperated noise.

"Whatcha doing?" asked Marco. He was sitting in a chair by the window, soaking up sunlight. Their mom had thrown a fit when he wanted to get out of bed, as if a few feet would mean the difference between sick and well, but Marco had won. He always won, when he wanted to.

"Journaling," said Gabby. "For school."

"Can I see?" asked Marco. Gabby shook her head. Marco sat forward. "Come on, Gabs."

She clutched the journal to her chest. *"No."*

She knew what she was doing was wrong — the lies had started small and taken on a life of their own — and if Marco saw what she'd written, the lies she'd told about him, he'd be angry. Or worse, he'd be hurt. She expected Marco to make a grab for the journal — there was a time he would have snatched it right out of her hands — but he simply shrugged and sank back into his chair.

"I have a journal," he said quietly.

Gabby's eyes widened. "Really?"

He gestured to the blue-and-white-striped book Gabby had given him the day before school started. "I started writing in it right after you gave it to me."

"What do you write about?" asked Gabby.

Marco shrugged. "All kinds of things. I write about life before getting sick. Mostly I write about being stuck in the hospital and the strange and random things I notice here. And of course I write about Henry and Mom and you."

"You write about me?"

"Sure. You want to see?"

Gabby found herself nodding. Marco's mouth twitched up tiredly. "A page for a page," he said.

Gabby's heart sank as she shook her head. "I can't."

Marco shrugged. "Fine," he said, tipping his head back and closing his eyes. Stretched out in the puddle of sun, he looked so . . . normal. Sometimes *normal* felt so far away, but looking at him now, she wanted to believe it could happen.

Gabby got to her feet.

"If you ever change your mind," he added as she reached the door. "Let me know."

"Sure," said Gabby softly as she slipped into the hall and went in search of Aria.

Gabby could hear her friend's laughter — it carried, even when she wasn't loud — from halfway down the hall. She was in Henry's room. Gabby heard Henry make a small, laughlike noise, too.

Gabby stopped and peered through the glass and saw Aria sitting there, cross-legged in Henry's wheelchair. She was about to open the door, when she heard Henry ask, "What are *your* parents like?"

And Aria simply said, "I don't have any."

Gabby's stomach twisted. She'd assumed . . . well, she didn't know what she'd assumed. Aria had said it was complicated, and Gabby had let it go. Maybe she'd known, deep down, been able to sense that hole, and stepped around it. But now that she knew, she could feel the pity rising in her chest. The same pity she couldn't stand from other people.

If Henry felt sorry for Aria, it never showed in his voice. "We're all missing pieces," he said. And then his voice lowered, and he added, "Can I tell you something?"

Gabby hesitated. She knew she shouldn't keep eavesdropping, but she couldn't bring herself to leave, or to interrupt him, not once Aria said, "Of course."

Gabby chewed her lip, and pressed her ear against the door.

"Sometimes," he said, "I feel like I spend all day bracing myself for when my parents come."

"You don't want them to?" asked Aria.

"I love them," said Henry. "I really, really love them. But I sometimes think that if they didn't come, if I didn't have to see the pain and the hope in their eyes every single day then I could just . . ." He sighed.

"Just what?" asked Aria.

"I've been sick since I was eleven," he said. "And at first, they thought I could get better, it looked like I might, but eventually . . . it was just a matter of time. The *gift of time*, that's what they call it, when you're not going to get better. They give you a prediction — maybe a few weeks, maybe a few months, maybe even a year — and they call it a gift. I was fourteen when the doctors gave me their prediction.

"Eight months," he said, clearly worn out from talking but determined to keep going. "That's what they said. And I held on, every day, every week, every month, for my parents. And when those eight months were up, I just . . . kept holding on. For them. Still not getting better. Still not getting worse. And every day my family would come and I'd still be here and it would be this miracle. And for a while, it was worth it, for the hope it brought them. But . . ."

Henry's voice tightened and he trailed off. Gabby and Aria both waited for him to go on, but he didn't. Gabby's heart ached. She hadn't known how long Henry had been sick, or that he would never get better. Did Marco know?

"Hey, what's your favorite color?" asked Aria, breaking the silence.

Henry seemed relieved to change the subject. "It used to be yellow," he said, "before they moved me to this hall." Gabby looked around and saw the walls were indeed a faded lemon color. "But now I can't get away from yellow. So it's red."

Aria smiled. "Close your eyes."

"What?"

"Trust me."

What was Aria up to? wondered Gabby. She peered in through the glass as Henry closed his eyes, and Aria tilted her head, as if thinking, and a moment later, something happened: the blanket on Henry's bed *changed color.* Gabby gaped. That wasn't possible. Aria hadn't moved, hadn't *done* anything, but instead of a dull cream fabric, the blanket was now a vibrant crimson red. Gabby hadn't blinked, hadn't looked away for a second, so how had Aria done it?

Gabby remembered that when Marco was eight or nine, he announced he was going to be a magician. He wasn't very good, but Gabby was very gullible, falling for every one of his tricks. But she was older now, and she knew there was no such thing as magic. Coins were hidden up sleeves and in pockets, and fast fingers could make things disappear. But Aria didn't have long sleeves on, and even if she did, she couldn't hide a *blanket* in them!

Gabby started to think she'd imagined the new color, but when Henry opened his eyes and looked down, he let out a small, delighted sound. He obviously saw it, too.

"How on earth did you do that?" he asked, running his hand over the fabric as if the color might rub off. *It wasn't like a magic* trick, thought Gabby. *It* was —

"Magic," said Aria.

"No such thing," said Henry, still touching the blanket in disbelief.

Aria shrugged her shoulders playfully. "Hey," she said. "Why don't you come hang out with us? Me and Gabby and Marco? It'll make you feel better."

At that, the tiredness slid back into Henry's face. "You go on," he said. "I'll try to swing by later."

Gabby came to her senses and backed away from the door just in time to avoid colliding with Aria as she came out.

"Oh, hey," said Aria brightly.

Gabby's mind was still spinning as she said, "Oh, hi! You want to um . . . go . . . get some food . . . or . . .

something . . . ?" Gabby wanted to bang her head against a wall. She sounded like an idiot. This was *Aria*. Aria was strange and apparently capable of ridiculously believable magic tricks, but she was still Aria.

"Sure," said Aria.

It was only after they'd raided the third vending machine — Aria was fascinated by the way they worked — that Gabby remembered the part of the conversation about Aria's parents. Is that why she liked to come over to Gabby's place all the time? Aria was so cheerful, so loud, that Gabby hadn't thought about the fact she might be hiding from something, too.

"I know this is random, and we have school tomorrow," Gabby said, "but do you want to spend the night?"

Aria's eyes lit up. "I'd love that."

They loaded their vending machine bounty into Aria's backpack, and set out.

"Hey," said Aria when they were halfway to Gabby's apartment. "Do you believe in magic?"

Gabby's heart raced. Had Aria seen her spying? Or was she simply asking one of her strange questions?

"I don't know," said Gabby after a long pause. "I'd have to see it to believe it."

But even then, she wondered, would she?

chapter 16

ARIA

One moment Aria was lying in a nest of blankets on Gabby's floor (thinking about how nice it was to be visible and comfy instead of invisible and afraid of being heard) and the next she was being trampled by a very flustered Gabby as she leaped out of bed with a panicked cry and nearly landed on top of her.

"What's wrong?" asked Aria as Gabby mumbled a quick apology and kept going, gathering up clothes before dashing out into the hall.

"The permission slip," called Gabby, turning on the shower in the bathroom. "I forgot to get it signed!" The door slammed and almost immediately reopened. "How fast can you get ready?" she called.

"Two minutes," said Aria, even though she really needed only two seconds, but that would have been hard to explain.

"Great," said Gabby. The door shut. And then reopened. "You can borrow some of my clothes!" It shut again and stayed closed.

Aria got to her feet and went to peruse Gabby's closet, thinking about how easy it would be if they just used her shadow to get to the hospital. It would just take a moment, and the truth was, Aria was getting tired of hiding her secret from Gabby. There was nothing *stopping* Aria from telling her, no force like the one that had kept her out of the apartment. It was just the fear that sharing her secret would make things worse when they were finally starting to get better.

"Are you almost ready?" called Gabby.

"Yeah, coming," said Aria, tugging a blue shirt off its hanger.

They half walked, half jogged to the hospital, Gabby slowing only when she finally reached the lobby.

"See?" said Aria, breathless. "Plenty of time to spare."

"Wait here," said Gabby. "I'll be right back."

Aria nodded and perched on the edge of a chair while Gabby disappeared down the hall. Aria pulled her own permission slip from her bag, and stared at the blank space where a parent was supposed to sign. She wondered absently what it would be like, to have a family, to have a name to fill in the box.

"What's *your* name?" she asked a woman sitting in a chair next to her. The woman looked surprised, but answered, "Delilah."

"That's very pretty," said Aria. She was halfway through filling in the blank — *Delilah Blue* — when a strange tug formed in her chest. It was the kind of inexplicable pull that normally drew her to Gabby, but this one was tugging her in another direction. She got up and followed the pull left beyond the desk and up two flights, frowning as she realized where she was going.

Henry's room.

She was halfway to his door when it opened, and a couple stepped out into the hall. They looked like Henry, minus the sickly pale. *Parents*, thought Aria, as they turned and walked away. They did it so slowly, as if wearing weights. Aria waited until they were gone before she peered through the glass and saw Henry in bed, the red blanket spread across his lap (she'd wanted to give him something he could put away so he wouldn't fall out of love with the color). He seemed so *sad*. His expression was raw, unguarded, and since Aria could tell that the sadness was something he wore only when he was alone, and since it seemed wrong to see it without his permission, she knocked.

"Aria," he whispered as she stepped in.

"Hey, Henry."

"I'm really glad you're here," said Henry. Something was different about him. The dark purple smoke that usually hung like a cloud around him had come unstuck and now swirled in the air above him. "I said good-bye to my parents today. They don't know it, but I did."

"What do you mean?" she asked.

"I'm tired. . . ." He closed his eyes. "So are they."

Aria thought about something Gabby had said to her, about the fact that Marco may be the one in bed, but they were all ill. Sickness did that, infected everyone. But that no one could get better until the one in bed did.

"Your parents won't get better," said Aria. "Not until you do."

There was a long, long pause. "I know," said Henry. He closed his eyes.

Aria got to her feet and was nearly to the door when she heard him whisper.

"Thanks, Aria," he said. "For listening."

"You're welcome, Henry," she whispered back before slipping out.

And then, halfway down the hall, Aria passed a teenage boy.

She almost didn't notice him, but the jingle of his bracelet snagged her attention. He was tall and slim, with black hair and eyes the prettiest green she'd ever seen, and he was wearing a charm bracelet. It was a bruised purple, almost black, but unlike Aria's bracelet, his wasn't bare. On it hung a handful of dark pendants in the shape of feathers.

The boy smiled a faint, sad smile as he passed by her. Aria thought she'd be relieved to see him, but a sinking feeling filled her chest as she watched him make his way toward Henry's room and go inside.

chapter 17

GABBY

Gabby found her mom in the hall talking to a nurse.

"What are you doing here, *mija*?" asked Mrs. Torres. "Shouldn't you be on your way to school?"

"I need you to sign a permission slip, so I can join a club." Gabby unfolded the paper and smoothed it out a little before handing it over.

"What club?"

"Choir," she said.

"That's wonderful," said her mom. "I'm always saying you have a lovely voice."

Gabby hadn't heard her mom say anything like that in years. In fact, on the rare occasion Mrs. Torres heard her daughter humming, she usually shushed her. But Gabby simply nodded and took the sheet back. She was about to leave when she hesitated and said, "I really like this school."

"I'm glad," said her mom, her attention already sliding away.

"I hope we can stay," added Gabby. "I mean, not that I hope Marco has to stay *here* that long, of course, but I hope that after . . . when he's better . . ."

"One step at a time," said her mom. "We shouldn't look over the hill until we reach the top. Marco needs to focus all his energy on getting better."

"I'm not talking about Marco, I'm talking about *me*." Gabby cringed as soon as she said it.

"*Gabrielle Torres* —" scolded her mom.

"I'm sorry," she said. "I didn't mean it like that. I know we're here for Marco. But what's so wrong with having something to look forward to?" Gabby didn't know if she was talking about Marco right now or herself. She decided she should be talking about Marco, so she added, "The high school's right next to the middle school, and it has an awesome soccer team, and —"

Mrs. Torres's phone rang, cutting her off. She held up a hand. "We'll talk about this later, *mija*."

Gabby sighed and nodded, even though she knew they wouldn't.

She headed back to the lobby, but Aria wasn't there.

Gabby was about to go looking for her when the girl suddenly appeared.

But for the first time since they'd met, Aria didn't seem very happy. In fact, she looked a little shaken up.

"You okay?" asked Gabby. Aria blinked a few times and forced something that was almost a smile but wasn't.

"Yeah, sorry," she said. "Did your mom sign the paper?"

Gabby waved the permission slip. "We're good to go," she said. And then she wondered who had signed Aria's paper. If her parents weren't around, then who did she live with? Now didn't seem like the right time to ask.

Even though they chatted on the way to school, Gabby was good enough at reading people to see that something was definitely on Aria's mind. All morning she seemed off, and when she wasn't herself by lunchtime, Gabby finally spoke up.

"What's going on?" she asked. "Is something wrong?"

Aria shook her head. "No," she said. "I'm sorry . . . it's nothing . . . I just . . ." She shook her head again, as if trying to shake away a thought and brightened forcibly. "Cookies. We need cookies. I'll go get us some."

And before Gabby could say anything, Aria vanished back into the lunch line. Gabby stood there with her tray and turned to survey the lunchroom. It had seemed so scary on the first day, when everyone was a stranger and every table a foreign territory, but now it didn't look so frightening. She recognized half the faces, and —

"Hey!" called Charlotte from a table across the cafeteria. "Over here!"

Gabby glanced around, worried she must be signaling to someone else, but Charlotte called out again, this time saying, "Hey, Gabby!"

The short boy with the soccer ball — Sam — was sitting beside her, and they waved Gabby over.

She made her way up to their table, tray in hand, and Sam kicked his backpack off the chair beside him so Gabby could sit.

"Hey there," he said. "I'm Sam."

"I know," said Gabby. "I'm Gabby Torres."

"Listen to you," said Sam with a whistle. "Giving your full name. Just like a star."

Gabby blushed. She'd gotten used to saying her last name because at the hospitals — and everywhere else, before now — she existed in relation to Marco. He was a patient. She was a family member. The last name was how they placed her.

"He's just teasing you," said Charlotte. "And besides, it's a compliment! Got to have a good stage name." She twirled her ponytail. "My last name's Bellarmine, but if I make it big I'm going by Bell. Charlotte Bell."

"Charlie Bell," said Sam, "and it's only a matter of when, not if."

Gabby's chest tightened. *Ifs* and *whens* ruled Marco's life.

"You're a quiet one, Gabby Torres," said Sam.

Gabby shook her head. "Sorry," she said. "Sometimes I forget I'm not speaking."

"Internal monologue," said Charlotte. "That's what it's called."

"Really?" asked Gabby. "Well, my . . ." She almost said brother, but stopped. She didn't know why she stopped, hated herself for stopping, but she couldn't do it, couldn't will herself to drop Marco into this like a weight. "My mom is always reminding me to speak up."

Two lies. It was her brother who said those kinds of things, not her mom. Because her mom would never notice.

"I bet my mom wishes I had that problem," rambled Charlotte. "She says my voice may be a gift, but the fact I use it so much isn't."

"You're a really good singer," said Gabby.

Sam ruffled Charlotte's hair. "Understatement, Gabby Torres. Charlie here is *amazing*."

Charlotte blushed and shrugged. "I like singing, but I really want to be an actress."

"She'd be president of the theater club," said Sam, "but they won't let a person in her position . . ."

"What position?" asked Gabby.

"Seventh grade," Charlotte groaned. "It's not my fault I'm an old soul trapped in a seventh grader's body."

Sam laughed. Gabby smiled. And then a crash echoed across the cafeteria, and all three turned to see Aria standing there, a wall of cookies and chips overturned at her feet.

chapter 18

ARIA

Aria had been hiding behind the snack shelf.

She'd seen Charlotte and Sam the moment she and Gabby had reached the cafeteria. More important, she'd seen Charlotte and Sam see *Gabby*, and she'd spent the last several minutes pretending to examine the school's dessert selection while secretly watching the trio. And watching Gabby's *smoke*. As Gabby sat down and chatted and smiled, her smoke began to twist. And then it began to thin. A lot.

Aria had been so excited to see it that she'd leaned forward into the shelf, and before she knew it, the whole thing had come crashing down. She stood there a moment, stunned by the hundreds of eyes that looked her way. So this was what the opposite of invisible felt like.

After a second, the kids turned back to their lunch, and

Aria shook off the surprise and stepped gingerly over the mess as she approached Gabby's table.

Aria said hi, and Sam and Charlotte said hi back, and Sam mentioned that everything on Aria's plate was purple — it was — and then a strange thing happened. Aria had been worried that Charlotte and Sam might gravitate toward her instead of Gabby, but she was wrong. In fact, they hardly seemed to notice her. Their attention kind of . . . slid off, drawn back to Gabby. It didn't hurt Aria's feelings. On the contrary, it made things better. Easier. After all, Aria couldn't stay. Sam and Charlotte could.

Aria reached for her drink, and her bracelet knocked against a bowl on her tray. She frowned, thinking about the boy in the hall, and the feather charms hanging from his wrist. Is that how wings were earned? One feather at a time? Would that boy get a new feather for helping Henry? What kind of help had Henry needed?

"I have to ask," said Gabby, and Aria dragged her attention back to the table. "What's with the soccer ball?"

"Here we go," said Charlotte, rolling her eyes.

Sam let it fall forward onto the table and rested his elbow on top. "I read somewhere that athletes, the really great ones, keep their ball with them wherever they go. They bond with it and —"

"That is so utterly ridiculous," cut in Charlotte.

"I don't know," said Gabby. "My brother tried it for a week once." Her mouth snapped shut as soon as she said it.

"You have a brother?" asked Charlotte.

"Yeah," she said slowly. "He's in high school."

"What position does he play?"

Gabby picked at her food. "He was a defender."

"Was?" asked Charlotte, clearly worried.

"He's taking a season off," Gabby said quickly. "He got injured." Aria frowned at the lie, even though she understood why Gabby did it. She didn't want Charlotte and Sam to look at her differently because of Marco, but still . . .

"What position do you play?" Aria asked Sam.

"Sam is, in fact, a horrible goalie."

"Charlotte!"

"Dude, no offense, but you're, like, four feet tall."

"I'm waiting for my growth spurt."

Gabby smiled despite herself. Charlotte snorted. Aria chuckled. Sam ignored them all.

"I want to be as good as possible. Hey, Gabby, maybe your brother could give me some pointers."

"Yeah," Gabby said quietly. "Maybe."

"Sports are boring," offered Charlotte. "Back to music. I can't wait to hear you audition, Gabby."

Gabby nearly spit out her drink. "Do what?"

"Audition," said Charlotte. "You know, so Ms. Riley can assign solos. You didn't think we just sat around harmonizing in a circle all the time, did you?"

"I . . . I wasn't sure. . . ."

"Don't worry," said Sam, resting his chin on his soccer ball. "You'll do great."

Aria watched as Gabby's smoke twisted and curled with doubts. Other people believed in her, and that had made a dent, but she needed to believe in herself. And Aria knew that wasn't something she or Charlotte or Sam or anyone could do for her.

"I just don't know if I'm ready to sing alone," said Gabby. "I'm not that good."

Sam squinted. "Are you doing that thing people do when they know they're good and just want to be told?"

"Sam," said Charlotte soberly, "I think she's being serious. Are you being serious? Because you're good. Like, really good. You sure you've never really sung before?"

Gabby shook her head.

"You don't need voice lessons. You need *voice* lessons."

"I . . . I don't know the difference," said Gabby.

Charlotte took a long, dramatic breath. "I mean

confidence. You know how to sing. But you can't sing your best until you know what your voice is."

"Until you're a *who*!" chimed in Aria. All three looked at her. "Until you know who you are," she clarified.

"Yeah, exactly," said Charlotte, nodding firmly. The bell rang overhead. "So the question, Gabby Torres, is: Who are you?"

chapter 19

GABBY

M s. Riley smiled when Gabby came in.

"So glad you decided to stay," she said, collecting the permission slips.

Gabby managed a small, nervous smile. She hoped she would be, too.

Choir started the way it had on Friday, with the warm-ups in the circle, but after only a couple of songs, Ms. Riley announced it was time to audition for solos. Gabby's stomach began to twist, and she forced herself to take a few steadying breaths.

Each student, Ms. Riley explained, would get up on the small stage that ran down one side of the room and perform for the rest of the group. They could pick any song they wanted, but there would be no musical accompaniment. Just voices.

"A word," she said, "before we get started. Singing isn't just about notes or lyrics. It's about the things between the words, the pieces of song that don't go on paper. When you sing, you shouldn't be reciting. You should be infusing. It's about expression — Mr. Robert is fond of that phrase, isn't he? Only here, you don't have to find the words. I can give you those. But you have to find the heart."

Charlotte rolled her eyes playfully.

She was up first. And Gabby thought she was fabulous. Her voice was lovely and clear, like bells. *Blue* came after *Bellarmine*, and Aria took the stage next. Gabby knew she was only here for her and she felt kind of bad about getting her into this . . . and then she remembered that she *hadn't*. The whole thing had been Aria's idea.

Aria cleared her throat and started to sing. Gabby smiled when she recognized the song. They must have heard it a dozen times on the radio. And Aria wasn't that bad. She even found the right key once or twice, and when it was over she mimicked Charlotte's bow, and the class gave a dappled applause as she stepped off the miniature stage.

"What do you think?" Aria asked Gabby as she took her seat. "Am I destined to be a star?"

"Definitely," said Gabby. And she meant it. Aria probably didn't have a future as a singer, but she was bright, and she made everything around her brighter. It was weird, thought Gabby, that no one else seemed to notice.

They continued down the roster, until Ms. Riley reached the letter *T*, and Gabby knew what that meant. It was her turn.

"Miss Torres, you're up."

She felt a little ill as she got to her feet and approached the makeshift stage. She knew what she wanted to sing, but as she got up on the platform and turned to face the room, her mouth went dry. The students stared at her, waiting. Ms. Riley stared at her, waiting. The only one who didn't stare at her, waiting, was Aria, because Aria was suddenly nowhere to be seen. Gabby frowned. Had she chosen now of all times to go to the bathroom? Just then, Charlotte whistled, and Sam clapped, the sounds dragging Gabby's attention back. She focused on Charlotte and Sam and started singing.

The first few notes tumbled out, timid and too soft, and Gabby faltered to a stop. In that moment she wanted nothing more than to stop and get off the stage, to hide. Everyone was *listening* and that was terrifying, so Gabby did the only thing she could think of.

She closed her eyes.

And it was funny, but she could almost feel a hand on her shoulder, and the weight of it was calming. She took a deep breath and started again, and whether it was the closed eyes or the imaginary hand, this time, the song came easily.

It was an old song, the kind her *abuela* used to hum, the kind her mom had even hummed back before she'd stopped humming and started stressing, the kind Gabby usually hummed to herself when she was alone, the melody gentle, comforting.

Gabby had to drag the lyrics out of the back of her mind because it had been so long since she'd actually sung them. The melody lived in her head all the time, but the words were tucked away.

But they came to her now, and she sang, and with her eyes closed she forgot that she was singing them to anyone but herself. And then the song ended, and she heard clapping, and blinked to find the whole room applauding. Charlotte and Sam — and Aria, back in her seat like she'd never left — the loudest.

"Brill," said Charlotte, patting her arm as Gabby took her seat, trembling a little.

"Told ya," said Sam.

"You were *great*," added Aria.

Relief and happiness swirled inside Gabby. It felt . . . amazing. To be seen this way. Knowing that none of the attention had to do with Marco's sickness. It didn't have to do with Marco at all.

It belonged to her.

It made her feel, as Aria had said, like a *who*.

The happiness followed Gabby all the way to the hospital. She didn't even mind that Aria was still being quiet, because for once, Gabby felt loud. She couldn't wait to tell Marco about the singing. She knew he'd be proud of her. But when she was nearly at his room, she drew up short.

Something was wrong.

She could hear someone shouting. No, she could hear *Marco* shouting.

But Marco *never* shouted. He hardly ever even raised his voice.

She hurried toward the noise. Aria said something but Gabby ignored her. She reached the door just in time to hear a water glass shatter against it from the other side.

A nurse was hurrying down the hall with a capped syringe in hand, and Gabby grabbed her sleeve. "What's going on?"

"Oh, his friend," said the nurse. "I'm afraid he . . ." She didn't finish, and Gabby didn't need her to.

Her stomach twisted. *Henry*. How had it happened? When had it happened?

Beyond the door, Gabby heard her mom trying desperately to calm Marco down, a stream of soothing Spanish pouring from her lips. But Marco pitched the nearest thing — a book — at the wall and beat his fists against the bed and screamed about how it wasn't fair. None of it was fair. And when Mrs. Torres reached for him, he pushed her away, then buried his face in his pillow as he sobbed.

Gabby wanted to go in, to go to him, wanted to wrap her arms around him and tell him it would be okay. But maybe it wouldn't be. Maybe none of this would be okay. It *wasn't* fair. Life wasn't fair. Death wasn't fair, and nothing Gabby could say right now would make it any easier to bear. Marco was upset, and he *deserved* to be upset. No one in this hospital was ever upset enough. They all treated death like a sad routine instead of a tragedy.

Gabby felt Aria wrap her arms around her shoulders, and she stood there numb, watching her brother rail in his room until the nurses gave him something and he went quiet — quiet, but not calm — and she couldn't bear to see that.

So she pulled away from Aria's grip and escaped to a bench at the end of the hall, sank onto it, and sobbed.

chapter 20

ARIA

Aria had been dreading it all day.

She knew it was coming. Maybe not *all* of her knew it, but part of her knew. Part of her knew as soon as she saw the teenage boy in the hall that morning. As soon as she saw the color of his smoke.

Knowing didn't make it any easier.

Aria hovered, caught between the quieting sadness in Marco's room and the growing sadness at the end of the hall, leaving Gabby alone for a few minutes until her crying subsided.

"I'm sorry," Aria finally whispered as she slid onto the bench beside her.

"What if he was alone?" Gabby's voice trembled a little as she wiped her eyes on her sleeve. "When he died?"

"He wasn't," said Aria, too quietly for Gabby to hear.

"It's not fair," whispered Gabby, balling her hands into fists. "None of this is fair."

Aria looked up at the ceiling and wished it were the sky. "At least he's —"

"Don't," snapped Gabby. "Don't say at least he's at peace now. I hate it when people say that like it makes death better."

"I don't think anything makes death better," said Aria. "But it was time for —"

"It's never just *time*," said Gabby. "And how can you say that?" She shook her head. "I thought you cared about him. . . ."

"I did," said Aria. "I *do*. But Henry was . . . I think he wanted to let go."

Gabby gave her a long hard look. "You knew."

Aria's eyes widened. "What?"

"All day you've been weird. You knew this was going to happen. Or that it *had* happened."

Aria could feel it. This cusp. The chance to tell Gabby the truth.

"You were with him before school, weren't you?" pressed Gabby. "That's where you ran off to. Did something happen? How did you know?"

Aria sighed. She was so tired of keeping secrets. Would it make Gabby feel better, to know Henry hadn't been alone?

To know it was time for him to let go? To know why Aria was here?

"I saw him come this morning," she said quietly.

"Saw who?"

Aria chewed her lip. "The boy in the hall. I'd been waiting for him. He was a different kind of . . ." She trailed off.

"Of what?"

Aria didn't actually like this word. It seemed too large, too heavy, but it was the only way she knew to explain. "Angel."

She'd braced herself for any number of reactions to the too-big word, everything from disbelief to mockery to awe. But Gabby only stared at her, eyes red.

"A what?" she whispered.

"An angel," said Aria again. "Like me. I wasn't sent to help Henry, though," she added. "I only noticed him because of the smoke. He was surrounded by this dark purple cloud. It's a marking, a flag for someone . . . someone like me but not me, and for some reason no one else had come, so I tried to keep an eye on him until they did. And now I think they didn't come because he just wasn't ready for *their* help, wasn't ready to let go. Like I said, he needed a different kind of . . ." Aria trailed off.

Gabby was staring at her, horrified. "If you didn't come for Henry, then why are you here? Is it Marco? Did you come because . . . oh god, is he going to —"

"I didn't come for Marco, either," said Aria. "I came for you."

Gabby's eyes widened. "Am *I* going to die?"

Aria sighed. "I told you, I'm not *that kind* of angel. I'm a . . . a guardian. I'm here to help you."

"I don't need your help," said Gabby. "Marco does."

Aria shook her head. "I can't help *him*," she said. "Not that way. I'm not a healer."

"So you came here just to do *what*?" snapped Gabby, the smoke coiling around her. "Offer moral support?"

"I can't fix people, Gabby."

"But you just said you're an angel."

"I know, but . . ."

"You said you're an *angel*," repeated Gabby, her voice clawing up, traveling down the hall. "Angels do miracles. Angels fix people. *Angels make things better.* If you're an angel, then make this better. Make Marco better. And if you can't, then *just go away*."

Aria pulled back, struck by the words. Her eyes began to burn, and before the tears could spill over, she disappeared.

chapter 21

GABBY

Gabby stared at the place Aria had been, feeling flushed and breathless.

Good, she thought bitterly as she got to her feet. *Run away*. Gabby didn't know what Aria was — or how she'd disappeared — but she wasn't an angel. She couldn't be. Gabby didn't know if she even believed in angels, but if she did, and they were real, they would be able to help her brother. Aria couldn't.

A tired sadness came over Gabby.

Her mom was pacing up and down the hall on the phone, and she didn't look up, let alone notice Gabby, as she slipped inside Marco's room.

He was lying on the bed facing the wall with his back to the room, clutching his pillow. She could tell he wasn't asleep by the way his chest rose and fell, his rib cage expanding and contracting too much through his shirt.

Gabby kicked off her shoes and climbed onto the bed beside him. Marco didn't say anything, didn't even look over his shoulder, but he scooted forward a few inches on the narrow bed to make room for her. She brought her hand to rest on her brother's shoulder, and she felt him take a small, shuddering breath.

"I'm sorry," she whispered, even though she hated the way people tossed around that phrase in hospitals. But she really, really was.

Marco had known Henry for only a few short weeks, but the two had hit it off so quickly. When she'd asked them about it, Henry had shrugged in his usual, easy way.

"When you're sick," he'd said, "and you don't know how much time you have, it's easy to make friends. You don't sit around and weigh the pros and cons, or wonder if you have enough in common. It's a waste of time, so you just say, 'Hey, I'm stuck here, you're stuck here, let's hang out.'"

And it *had* been easy. Even though everyone could see Henry was sick, and Gabby could see he was sad, he'd brought a kind of light with him, wherever he went.

And now he was gone. And Marco was lost. And Aria had run away.

Strangely, Gabby's mind went to her journal. Why couldn't life be like she'd written it? Marco should be out playing soccer and Henry should be in the stands cheering for him, and instead they were here and he was gone and Aria . . . Gabby didn't even know where to start with Aria.

When Marco rolled over to face her sometime later, his eyes were feverish.

"*¿Dónde estás?*" he whispered. *Where are you?*

"I don't know," she whispered back.

"I heard you shouting," he said. "Who were you fighting with?"

"Aria."

"Why?"

Gabby realized she couldn't answer, in part because it would sound ridiculous — *my new best friend turned out to be an angel who can't save you* — and in part because that wasn't a fair reason to be mad at Aria. But she was mad anyway because she wanted to be mad at someone.

"It's complicated," she said at last.

"Well, go fix it," said Marco.

"I can't," said Gabby. "I told her to go away, and she did."

"Look, whatever you're fighting about," said Marco. "It's

not worth it. Please, Gabs. I lost a friend today. Don't go throwing one away."

Gabby's heart ached. She knew he was right. "I don't know where she went," said Gabby lamely.

"So go find her," said Marco.

Gabby took a deep breath and nodded. She hugged her brother — he felt really warm — and then she got up and went to find Aria.

chapter 22

ARIA

Aria sank onto the hospital steps.

It wasn't her fault that she couldn't fix people. She *wanted* to fix them, and she would have used her power to do it if she could but . . . but she couldn't.

She was there to *help*, not fix.

Aria considered her bare charm bracelet, running her thumb over the three small, empty loops. She didn't seem to be doing a very good job of helping. She drew her knees to her chest and looked down at the dull gray hospital steps. She was tired of their sad gray paint, and thought that maybe, if the steps were a happier color, she'd feel happier, too. As soon as she thought it, color spread across the steps beneath her, overtaking the gray until each of the dozen stairs leading from the lot to the front doors was a different, vibrant hue. Stripes of blue and red and green and yellow. She felt her spirits rising a little at the bursts of color, until she remembered Gabby's words.

Angels do miracles.

Angels fix people.

Angels make things better.

What good was her magic if all she could do was change the color of some concrete? How was that making *anything* better? It wasn't a miracle. It was just a stupid magic trick.

She was about to change the steps back, when she heard a noise.

"Oooooooh," said an old, old woman being helped up the steps by a young man. "Ooooh, Eric, look!"

"That's nice, Nan."

The man tried to guide her up the steps, but she had come to a grinding halt. "They've painted the stairs!"

"I can see that, Nan."

"They've done it. Look at that. They've always been gray, and I'm always telling those doctors you can't paint a place like this gray. No good for anyone. I told them every time I came. Every time! And look!"

She beamed at Aria.

"Isn't it lovely?" the old woman asked her. "I told them, and look!"

Aria smiled a little and nodded. "They must have heard you," she said.

The old woman's head bobbed cheerfully as she continued up the steps, clutching the young man's arm and saying, "They heard me; they heard me."

Aria watched them go inside and decided to leave the steps the way they were. She closed her eyes and took a long, deep breath, and tried to remember the smile on the woman's face. And then she felt someone sit down on the step beside her.

It was Gabby.

Aria braced herself for another fight, but Gabby didn't scream, didn't snap, didn't say anything. She just sat there, looking pale. The blue smoke swirled around her, twisting and curling with questions.

"How long have you been an angel?" she asked.

"Nine days," said Aria.

Gabby made a small sound of surprise. "And before that?"

Aria frowned. "What do you mean?"

"I mean," said Gabby, casting a glance around, "were you dead?"

Ari crinkled her nose. "No. Of course not."

"Then how do you look like that?"

Aria looked down at herself. "Like what?"

"Like . . . well, like that," said Gabby, gesturing toward her. "Like someone who's been alive as long as I have."

Aria examined her hands, and shrugged. "This is what I've always looked like."

"For nine days."

"Should I look like someone else?" asked Aria.

"Can you?" asked Gabby.

Aria frowned. It had never occurred to her. She was happy with how she looked, since it was the only way she'd ever looked, but Gabby seemed curious, and that made Aria curious, too. She could change her clothes, but could she change herself?

Aria closed her eyes and tried to picture a new combination of features, different skin and different eyes and different hair.

"Well?" she asked, opening her eyes. "How do I look?"

Gabby shrugged. "You look the same."

And even though Aria acted like she was disappointed, she was secretly relieved that it hadn't worked. Silence fell again between them, heavy as a weight.

"If you're an angel," asked Gabby at last, "then where are your wings?"

Aria stiffened. "I don't have them *yet*," she said, a little defensively.

"So you can't fly."

Aria shook her head vigorously. "No," she said. "And trust me, I tried. It didn't go well."

Gabby's mouth twitched. "But you can disappear."

Aria nodded. "And I have a shadow."

"*Everybody* has a shadow," said Gabby.

"Yeah," replied Aria smiling a little, "but I'm pretty sure most shadows don't work like mine. Watch," she said, getting to her feet and turning so the sun struck her back and cast her shadow out in front of her. She looked down at the dark patch on the ground, pointed a finger, and said, sternly, "Stay."

Gabby looked at Aria the way any rational person would look at someone giving orders to their shadow. But the look slid from her face when Aria took a step back.

And her shadow didn't.

It stayed stock-still on the ground, as if caught in a game of freeze. Gabby's mouth fell open. And it stayed open when Aria snapped her fingers, and the shadow turned on like a light. Gabby's eyes widened in amazement.

That was the look Aria had hoped for when she told Gabby her secret.

"I don't need wings to get around," said Aria. "I have this."

"But what *is* it?" asked Gabby.

Aria considered the shape on the ground. "I guess it's a door."

"Where does it lead?"

Aria shrugged. "Depends on where I need to go."

Gabby bit her lip and looked at Aria's shadow and then at her own. Even though Aria couldn't read her mind, she could tell what she was thinking, as if the thoughts were words instead of smoke, swirling around her. She wanted to get away, to escape.

"Want to go somewhere?" asked Aria.

"Where would it take us?" asked Gabby.

Aria shrugged and held out her hand. "Let's find out."

chapter 33

GABBY

Aria made Gabby go first.

"Why?" asked Gabby nervously.

"Because," said Aria, "you want to know where it will take *you*. If I go first, it might get confused and take us somewhere else."

Aria squeezed Gabby's hand and guided her toward the light-filled shadow. Gabby tensed.

"Are you sure this will work?" Gabby asked.

"No," answered Aria. She started to say something else, but her voice was swallowed up as they stepped into the light.

It felt like falling but slower, like sinking in a pool. For a moment there was nothing. And then, quick as a blink, there was something. Or rather, *somewhere*.

Gabby looked around. She didn't know what she'd expected. Half of her thought that since it was a *magical* shadow, she'd end up somewhere magical. The other half thought the door might take them to another version of her life. One where Marco wasn't sick. The kind of life she pretended was real when she was in school. And some small part of her thought that the shadow would take them to the woods behind her old house, the ones that haunted her dreams.

But it didn't. Aria's shadow took them to school. To the choir room.

"Why here?" asked Gabby.

Aria shrugged. "Maybe it's trying to tell you something. Maybe this place" — she looked around — "can help you." She ran her hand along the edge of the piano. "It's already starting to."

"What do you mean?" asked Gabby.

Aria perched on the piano bench. "Remember how I said Henry had been marked for someone, and you'd been marked for me? Well, that marking, it takes the shape of smoke. And when you feel like you don't matter, like you don't exist, like you're not a person, the smoke gets worse, because that's what your smoke is made of, those problems."

Gabby's eyes went to the floor, guilt rippling through her. "I shouldn't complain," she said. "They aren't real problems. Not compared to Marco's."

"I don't think it's a matter of *real*," said Aria, swinging her legs back and forth. "I think Marco's being sick, is a *loud* problem. So loud it makes every other problem seem quiet. And because they're quiet, you think they're less important. And maybe sometimes they are. But you have to ask yourself, if you didn't have his problems to compare yours to, would they really seem so quiet? Because I have to tell you, the fact that I'm here means your problems aren't quiet, or unimportant, or that they aren't *real*. They're very real. And the fact that I'm here means I can help."

"How?" asked Gabby, shaking her head. It was such a big question inside a small word. "No offense, Aria, but making things bright colors isn't going to help me."

"I think colors are *my* voice," said Aria. "Singing is yours." She tapped a few piano keys. "I wish you could see what happens when you sing," she said. "All that smoke, it gets thinner. Maybe that's why my shadow brought us here. Because this place, and the way it makes you feel, is a good direction. A future. One that belongs to *you*."

Gabby looked down at the floor. "But what about Marco?" she asked, that same old tightness working its way into her chest. "What about *his* future? Does he have one?"

Aria sighed. "I don't know what's going to happen to your brother," she said. "I wish I did, and I know it feels like everything depends on him. But that kind of thinking, it's the reason you forgot how to be you. This is your chance," she said, gesturing to the empty choir room. "And you're going to have to take it, Gabby. No matter what happens to Marco."

Gabby closed her eyes. She didn't want to picture her life *without* Marco. Could she picture her life *outside* of him?

She took a deep breath and opened her eyes and looked around the room. She pictured choir in session, Charlotte and Sam cracking jokes, the way the music lifted her up, the way the singing made her feel like *somebody*.

But at the hospital, she still felt like a ghost.

"They feel like two separate worlds," she blurted. "Here and the hospital."

"That's because they are," said Aria. "You've found your voice here. But you still don't have one there."

"What good is a voice when no one will listen?" whispered Gabby.

"If your mom were ready to listen," asked Aria, walking back toward her shadow, "would you be ready to talk?"

Gabby hesitated. She hadn't thought about it that way. She nodded. "Yes."

Aria smiled and held out her hand. "Then I'll see what I can do."

"Really?" asked Gabby, as she took Aria's hand.

"Hey," said Aria as the shadow beneath them turned on like a light, "I'm your guardian angel after all."

"Miss Torres," said Mr. Robert the next morning after class, "a word please."

Gabby tensed. She was nearly to the door when he said it. She looked back and saw that he was holding her journal. "This is good work," he said.

"Thanks," she said, turning again toward the door where Aria was waiting.

"There's only one problem," he said. Gabby's steps slowed and stopped. She felt dread wash over her. "My son goes to Grand Heights High," continued Mr. Robert. "He's one of the captains on the soccer team." Her heart sank as she turned back toward the teacher. "I asked him if he knew your brother. You can imagine my surprise when I found out Marco wasn't on the team. So I looked into it: he's not even enrolled at the school."

Gabby looked at the checkered linoleum floor.

"Why don't you tell me the truth?" said Mr. Robert.

She dragged her gaze up. Something in her crumpled. She was so tired of lying.

"My brother *would* be in tenth grade at Grand Heights High," she said. "And he *would* be the best player on the soccer team, but he's in the hospital. He's been sick for more than a year. We moved here so he could have surgery, but he got a cold and so it's on hold and we're all just stuck waiting and hoping he doesn't get worse, and I spend every moment thinking about it so I really don't want to talk about it, and I really don't want to write about it."

Gabby was breathless by the time she finished. She expected Mr. Robert to say he was sorry, to slip into that too-familiar mode of pity, of false kindness. But instead his brow crinkled.

"I'm going to make you a deal," he said. "You can write about anything you want in here, but it has to be true." He offered the journal back to her. "No more lies. Do you understand? Find a way to tell the truth."

Gabby took the journal and nodded.

"And I know it's none of my business," he added, "but I hope your brother gets better soon. Grand Heights High could use a few more great players."

Gabby almost smiled. "Please," she said, "don't tell anyone."

Mr. Robert shook his head. "It's not my story to tell," he said. "It's yours."

Maybe it *was* Gabby's story to tell, but she couldn't find the words to tell it.

She sat in Marco's hospital room that afternoon, staring at a blank page.

It wasn't that Gabby didn't know what to say. Dozens of thoughts spiraled through her mind, about Marco and Henry and Aria and school and the hospital. But she was afraid that if she started, she wouldn't be able to stop, just like in the classroom when she'd spilled out her thoughts to the teacher.

Gabby wondered if the thoughts were filling her blue smoke, too. Aria said that's what the smoke was made of, things you felt and didn't say. But Aria was off wandering the hospital halls — she could never sit still — and Gabby couldn't ask her, and it wouldn't help her anyway because the page was still just as blank.

In a moment of frustration, Gabby lobbed her pen across the room.

"What did the pen ever do to you?" asked Marco. He was sitting in bed, head bent over his own journal. His face was flushed, and his temperature was up. Stress, a nurse had said, from losing Henry, but Mom was in a panic. She was meeting with the doctors right now.

"I don't know what to write," said Gabby.

"You've filled half the book," said Marco.

With lies, thought Gabby. "That was different," she said. "What are you writing about?"

Marco looked down at his page. "I'm not ready to write about *now*," he said. Gabby knew what he meant. He wasn't ready to write about Henry. "So I'm writing about when we were kids. Going to the beach. Growing up in that big house with the woods behind. It's easier. . . ." he said. "Maybe you should try that."

Gabby looked down at her blank page. She didn't want to write about now, either, but maybe she could write about before, too.

When we were younger, she started, *my brother and I used to race up the hill behind our house. . . .*

The line spilled out across the page, and Gabby let out a small sigh of relief (Mr. Robert was right, starting was the hardest part). Slowly, haltingly, she went on to describe the house and the yard and the woods. The way she and Marco raced, and the way Marco always won.

But when she got to the day he finally lost, the day they knew something was really wrong, Gabby stopped.

She didn't want to talk about that, but it felt good to write, so she jumped down a line, and started another story.

This one was about a camping trip they'd gone on last year, where her mom had gotten into a war with a squirrel. And when Gabby got to the point where Marco's sickness crept back into the story (they had to cut the trip short so he could go in for more treatment), she switched again. She did this, bouncing from story to story, cutting out the bits she didn't want to write (without filling in lies), making a patchwork of memories.

And with each story, she got a little closer to talking about *now*. It hovered at the edges. She even managed to write a little about how she was feeling, even if she wasn't ready to talk about why.

"Hey, Marco," she said when she'd filled five pages, "look how many —" But Marco had fallen asleep, the pen still in his hand, the journal open in his lap. Gabby slid silently to her feet and crossed to him.

Everything in her wanted to read the words on his page. But she didn't.

She reached out and closed his journal, careful not to wake him.

chapter 24

ARIA

Aria had examined the contents of every vending machine in the hospital and was on her way back to Marco's room with a selection of snacks when she rounded the corner and nearly ran into Mrs. Torres.

Gabby's mom didn't even seem to notice her.

"*No sé, no sé,*" she was saying into her phone. *I don't know, I don't know.* Aria marveled at the fact she understood the words. She put that solidly in the *pro* column of being an angel. The voice on the other line must have asked about Gabby because Mrs. Torres added, "Gabby's fine. She's always fine. She can take of herself."

Aria wanted to shake Mrs. Torres and tell her Gabby shouldn't have to take care of herself. But that wasn't the way to get rid of Gabby's smoke. Aria had to be clever.

If your mom were ready to listen, would you be ready to talk?

Yes, Gabby had said.

Aria just had to get Mrs. Torres to *listen.*

When Aria got to Marco's room, she peered in through the glass. He was asleep in his bed and Gabby was folded up in a chair, scribbling away in her journal.

That was it! Aria realized, pressing her face to the glass. She smiled. She had an idea.

That night, Aria lay awake on Gabby's floor, waiting for Mrs. Torres to come home.

Soon enough Aria heard the sound of the door open and then close. She heard the soft thuds of shoes being taken off and set by the door, then the scrape of a chair being slid across the floor, a body sinking into it.

Aria got to her feet and made sure she was invisible before wandering out into the apartment.

Mrs. Torres was sitting at the kitchen table.

She stared at the dark beyond the open window, her brown eyes so similar to Gabby's.

The simple fact was that even though Gabby was finding her voice, her mom still wasn't listening.

Aria couldn't make her listen. But maybe she could make her *read.*

Gabby's journal sat on the table a few inches from her mother's hand. Aria had made sure it was there before they went to bed.

Now she reached out an invisible hand, and flipped the journal open. Mrs. Torres looked down at the book and then to the open window, clearly wondering if there was a draft. Aria turned through a few more pages until she came across Gabby's newest entry. Aria had convinced Gabby to write it earlier that night. She told her she had to be honest, had to trust Aria, and Gabby had done both. Now Gabby's mom looked down at the page, at first absently, and then intently as she read the line at the top.

Some days I feel invisible.

Gabby's mom reached out and pulled the journal toward her.

I don't want to be the center of attention, continued the entry. *I just want to be seen.*

Aria held her breath. And then Mrs. Torres turned back to the first page of the notebook, and started from the beginning.

chapter 25

GABBY

The next morning, Gabby talked to a student in each of her classes. Once to ask for a pen, once to hand back a pen someone had dropped, and once just because she thought of something funny. It was getting easier, the talking.

Sam and Charlotte were waiting for her at lunch, and Gabby realized how happy she was to see them. She pictured the smoke Aria had talked about, imagined it thinning, and she could almost feel it, like a weight lifting.

Like a slice of blue sky through clouds.

But the best part of the day came in choir.

"Gather round," said Ms. Riley brightly. She held a crisp piece of paper, as if it were a prize. And then Gabby realized that it was. It was the choir concert roster.

"With the songs and the solos," whispered Sam beside her.

"I hope you get a solo," added Charlotte.

Gabby told herself she wouldn't, told herself it didn't matter, but then Ms. Riley read her name — *her name!* — and she felt herself breaking into a grin.

Excitement flooded through her, followed quickly by terror. The thought of singing in front of people made her queasy. She started to tell Ms. Riley to pick someone else, when Charlotte stopped her with a smile.

"You'll be great!" she said.

"Better than great," said Sam.

And then Aria wrapped her arms around her shoulders and squeezed. "You can do this," she said.

And for the first time, despite her fears, Gabby tried to believe her.

Afterward, Charlotte insisted they all go out for ice cream to celebrate.

"I don't know if I can," said Gabby automatically. She needed to be at the hospital with Marco . . . didn't she?

"Why not?" asked Charlotte.

"We won't be long," offered Sam.

"Just one scoop," added Charlotte. "You deserve it."

"You do," chimed in Aria. It was weird, but Gabby couldn't shake the feeling Aria had gotten quieter lately.

Gabby smiled sheepishly, then nodded. "Okay, but just one."

One scoop turned into two, which turned into three and a stomachache, but it was worth it, and as they sat on the benches outside the ice-cream shop, Gabby's mouth hurt from grinning. Sam and Charlotte were so easy to be around, so comfortable with each other.

"We've been next-door neighbors since we were really little," said Charlotte. "Would you believe there was a time when Sam was taller than me?"

Gabby laughed. "No way."

"I don't appreciate your skepticism," said Sam.

"Aw, it's okay, Sammie," said Charlotte. "Maybe you'll be tall again one day. Or at least average height."

The girls giggled. Sam scowled.

"How about you two?" asked Charlotte. "How do you and Aria know each other?"

Aria started to answer. "We met at the hos —"

"Apartment building," cut in Gabby, shooting Aria a look. "We moved in around the same time."

Aria's brow scrunched up, but she didn't contradict her. Gabby knew Aria didn't want her keeping secrets, and Gabby herself didn't want to keep them. It was just that she didn't want to talk about the hospital, not when things were going so well.

"That's awesome," said Charlotte. "To have a friend right there. Like a housewarming present."

Aria smiled. "Like fate," she said.

"Yeah," said Gabby, as she pulled the phone out of her pocket to check the time. Her stomach lurched when she saw the number of missed calls. She must have accidentally turned off the sound or something.

"Oh no," she said aloud, frantically accessing the three voice mails.

"What is it?" Charlotte asked.

"What's wrong?" Sam asked.

"Gabby?" Aria said softly.

Gabby pushed up from the bench as the voice mails played. They were all from her mom, and they were a blur of *Marco took a turn* and *tests came back* and *there's a problem* and *come to the hospital as soon as you can* and *where are you* and *where are you* and *where are you.*

Gabby tried to force air into her lungs, tried to breathe in that special calming way, but she didn't feel calm, only sick and dizzy as she grabbed Aria's arm and pulled her up from the bench with a rushed, "We have to get to the hospital *now.*"

"Wait, *hospital?*" asked Sam.

"Gabby, what's going on?" asked Charlotte.

"I'm sorry," Gabby mumbled, "I have to go. We have to go. I'm sorry."

She pulled Aria around the corner and took her by the shoulders and said, "Please, Aria. Take me there." And Aria didn't waste time asking questions. She stepped out of her shadow and she and Gabby hurried down into the light.

It was *the bad*.

Gabby's mom clutched Marco's hand as the doctor explained. Marco's fever had gotten worse, and by that morning he had a bad cough, too, so to be safe they'd run a panel and done some X-rays to make sure it wasn't pneumonia. It wasn't. It was *the bad*. There was a long word for what it had done — metastasized — which basically meant that the bad had snuck up into Marco's chest.

Gabby closed her eyes and pictured little pieces of it like crumbs, breaking off from Marco's leg and his hip and traveling through his blood to his lungs. She felt Aria's hand on her shoulder, even though the girl wasn't there. Or she was, she'd explained before she vanished, but Gabby wouldn't be able to see her.

"The good news," said the doctor, "is that we caught it very, very early. Your odds are still good. I can't lie and tell you they're as good as they were, but they're good. We'll operate as soon as possible and —"

"But you said it wasn't safe," cut in Gabby's mom. "You said we shouldn't operate while Marco was still sick. You said there was a higher risk of infection."

"There is," said the doctor, "but I'm afraid it's no longer safe to *not* operate. Every day we lose takes odds out of our favor."

"What now?" asked Marco, sitting forward. Gabby looked at him, the stubborn set of his jaw. She knew how much he wanted to get better, but she also knew how scared he was of the procedure. Before, there had been a chance he could lose his leg. Now, he could lose his life. And that was before the operation was even over.

"It's an extensive operation," said the doctor, "even more so now than before. We'll go in and excavate the affected bones in the left leg, as planned. At the same time, we'll need to go in through the chest and clear away the metastasized tumors. Even if everything goes well" — at the use of the word *if*, Gabby found Marco's eyes. He found hers. They held on to each other that way — "it's going to be a harder recovery."

Gabby's mom started to cry.

"I *still believe*," said the doctor, "that if the surgery is successful, the hardest part will be over. You won't be out of the woods, Marco, but you'll be on your way." And then, at last, the doctor turned toward Gabby. "Do *you* have any questions?"

Gabby's mind was nothing but questions: *Is Marco going to die? Is he going to be okay? What are his chances? What is going to happen? What can I do? What can any of us do? Why is this happening? Haven't we been through enough?* But the only one she actually asked was, "When is the surgery?"

The doctor tapped a pen against his clipboard. "Tomorrow morning."

"That soon?" asked Gabby's mom.

"Sounds good," cut in Marco. Mrs. Torres started to protest, but he cut her off. "The surgery was going to happen one way or another," he said. "It sucks that this is the reason it has to happen *now*, but I'm sick of waiting, and I'm sick of being sick, and the sooner I can get through this, *which I will*, the sooner I can get better, and get my life back." He finished, breathless and flushed, but his eyes were bright. "Okay?"

The doctor nodded. "All right, then. Let's help you get your life back."

Gabby focused on Aria's hand squeezing her shoulder and the strength in Marco's voice, and she tried to believe that everything would be all right.

chapter 26

ARIA

Gabby was sitting on the hospital steps with her head in her hands when Aria materialized beside her.

"Aria, please," said Gabby without looking up, "there has to be something you can do."

Aria's chest tightened at the plea. Not this again. If there was anything she could do for Marco, she would have done it already. "I told you, Gabby, I'm not a healer."

Gabby drew a shaky breath and looked up. And then her eyes widened.

"You said you saw smoke," she said, grabbing Aria by the shoulders. "Around Henry, before he died. Aria, you have to promise me you'll tell me if you see that kind of smoke around Marco. If you don't see it, then it means he'll be okay, right?"

Aria wished it were that simple, but she didn't think it was. After all, the hospital was filled with people, some of them who would be okay, and some who wouldn't, but those who wouldn't weren't all wreathed in a prophetic smoke. She worried that the smoke only marked Henry because he needed help letting go. What if Marco didn't?

"Gabby, I don't think —"

"Just promise me," begged Gabby. "If you see it, you'll tell me."

Aria sighed and nodded. "If I see it, I'll let you know."

Gabby made her shake on it. As Aria gripped Gabby's hand, she knew with a sinking heart that she would keep her word.

"Gabby?" called a voice, and the two pulled apart to see Sam and Charlotte trotting up the steps toward them.

"What are you doing here?" asked Gabby.

"You ran away talking about hospitals," said Charlotte, breathless. "We were worried."

"How did you know I was here?"

"We didn't. But there are only two hospitals in this area, and we already checked the other one."

Aria got to her feet. She took a step back and stood behind Gabby, watching as Sam and Charlotte sat down on either side of her.

"What's going on?" asked Sam.

And Aria watched proudly as Gabby took a deep breath and told them the truth. About the move. About Marco. Their eyes widened as they listened, but neither of them said anything. And when Gabby was finished, tears brimming and voice tight, Charlotte simply wrapped her arm around the girl's shoulders.

All day Gabby's smoke had been getting thinner. When she'd turned the journal in to Mr. Robert, it thinned. When she'd gotten the solo in choir, it thinned. When she'd laughed with Charlotte and Sam, it thinned. And despite all the hope and fear that came with the news about Marco, as Charlotte and Sam sat there comforting her, there was almost no blue left in the air. *This is right*, thought Aria, even as a strange sadness spread through her. *This is the way it's supposed to be.*

"Why would you hide something like that?" asked Charlotte at last.

"I just . . . I wanted a fresh start. I didn't want you to find out and feel like you had to be my friend out of . . . pity . . . or something."

"We wouldn't," said Sam simply.

"You don't know that," said Gabby, shaking her head.

"We would be *worried*," said Charlotte, "I mean, we *are* worried, but that's part of being someone's friend. We care about you."

Another wisp of smoke dissolved.

"What can we do?" asked Sam. "To help you."

Gabby chewed her lip. "Do you want to come say hi to Marco?"

"Is that a good idea?" asked Charlotte.

Gabby nodded. "I want you to meet him. I think he'll want to meet you."

"Then let's go," said Sam, bouncing his soccer ball. "And just so you know," he added as they made their way inside, Aria trailing behind, "we'd be your friends no matter what your family's like. My dad does Civil War reenactments, and Charlotte's parents decorate their house for every single holiday, even the silly ones. Plus her little sister is a monster in a tutu. But we're still cool."

"Way cool," said Charlotte.

"Super cool," said Gabby as she led them inside.

Aria followed in their wake, watching as more and more of the blue smoke disappeared.

chapter 27

GABBY

Gabby stood alone in the hallway.

Charlotte and Sam had just left, and Aria had gone in search of cookies, and Gabby was now staring through the glass insert of her brother's room. Marco had loved meeting her friends. He and Sam had talked for ages about soccer. Marco gave Sam a few pointers and said that being short could be a good thing out on the field. Charlotte, who was always so sure of herself, had been tongue-tied, not because of Marco's illness but because "he's really, really cute," she'd told Gabby in the hall. Gabby had screwed up her nose. "Ew."

Now they were gone, and Marco was resting and Gabby was standing outside his door, reading through her journal. She had started to go back through and write in the blanks between sections, filling in the things she'd been too scared to talk about before. It seemed important now, to put them down on paper. In case. As she read through what she'd written, she was amazed at how honest she'd become.

She didn't hear her mom come up beside her. When she noticed her, Gabby stepped out of the way instinctively to let her get to Marco.

But her mom didn't go in. She just stood there, next to Gabby, staring at her.

"*Mija*," she said. "I think . . . we should . . . I mean . . . we need to talk."

"About what?" asked Gabby, suddenly nervous. "Marco's surgery?"

Her mom's brow furrowed. "No . . . no, this isn't about Marco. This is about you."

"I didn't do anything."

"I didn't say you did," snapped her mom, and then, softening her voice, added, "I just want to know how you're doing. I want you to talk to me."

Gabby stared at her mom, as if the offer were a puzzle she needed to decipher. Part of her wanted to say no, to walk away. She'd waited for so long for her mom to ask, really ask, long enough that she'd stopped waiting. She'd given up. But wasn't that the problem? Wasn't that why Aria was here?

"I'm scared for Marco," Gabby said at last.

"I know," said her mom. "We both are. But right now I want to talk about *you*."

Gabby chewed her lip. "I like my school," she said at last. "I'm making friends and I don't want to leave, even if — *when* — Marco gets better. And I miss you," Gabby added, eyes burning. "I miss talking to you and I —"

She was cut off by the sound of her mom's phone.

Her heart sank as her mom pulled it out of her pocket. But her mom didn't answer it. Instead, she switched the ringer off.

"Go on," she said. "I'm here. And I'm listening."

chāpter 28

ARIA

Aria climbed the stairs, rounded the corner with her stack of cookies, and stopped.

There, at the other end of the hall, Gabby and her mom were sitting on a bench by the window, and they were *talking*. And as she watched, the very last of Gabby's smoke disappeared.

A strange sensation filled Aria's chest. She was proud and sad at the same time. This meant it was time to go. But she couldn't go yet, wouldn't go yet, not until after Marco's surgery. She'd promised to stay with Gabby, to let her know if she saw any smoke around her brother.

And Aria would keep her promise.

Later that night, in the hospital, everyone was asleep except for Marco and Aria.

Aria peered in through the glass insert and saw Mrs. Torres curled up on a cot in the corner and Gabby curled up on the chair, her notebook pressed to her chest. Marco was sitting up in a small pool of light, writing in his journal. And because people seemed to see Aria when she wanted to be seen, his gaze drifted to the door where she was standing, and he nodded for her to come in.

She padded silently into the room and sat in an empty chair beside his bed.

"Hi," he whispered.

"Can't sleep?" whispered Aria back.

Marco shook his head. "It's okay, though," he said softly. He hesitated, chewing the inside of his cheek. "I would rather be awake . . . while I can . . ." He looked at her for a long moment and said nothing. And then he added, "I'm glad Gabby has you, Aria."

Aria smiled, even though that same feeling tugged at her. The one that said Gabby didn't need her help anymore. That it was time to go.

"I hope I've been a good friend," she said, fiddling with the laces on her shoes (she'd made them red, for Henry). "This is all very new to me."

"Hospitals?"

"Everything."

"What do you mean?" asked Marco.

"I mean . . . I'm new to this . . . to being a person."

Marco squinted, confused, and Aria hesitated. It hadn't gone very well, the last time she told someone. But Gabby had been angry and scared when Aria told her, and Marco wasn't either of those things right now. "Want to know a secret?" she asked.

Aria leaned in and whispered what she was into his ear. Sharing a secret felt like a bit of magic, in that both magic and secrets change the people you share them with.

When Aria pulled back to see Marco's reaction, his eyebrows had gone up in surprise.

"You're joking," he said.

"I haven't really figured out how to joke yet," admitted Aria, and at that Marco laughed, then clasped a hand over his mouth to keep from waking anyone.

"Do you believe me?" she asked.

"Does it matter?" he asked, lowering his hand. She thought about that and was still thinking about it when Marco added, "I want to believe you. I like to think that Gabby has someone watching over her."

Aria tilted her head. "How do you know I'm not watching over *you*?"

Marco smiled a little. "Because I don't need you to." He

gestured to the room. "Everyone's already watching over me, looking out for me, trying to save me. Maybe they can; maybe they can't. But everyone's doing their best, and I'm doing my best, and I don't need you. . . ." The words could have sounded mean, but the way he said them wasn't mean at all. It was gentle. "I don't. But Gabby does. Besides, if you were here to save me, I bet you would have done it already."

Aria examined Marco.

"What is it?" he asked.

"I think in some ways," she said, "you're the healthiest one here."

"Tell the doctors that," he said with a grim smile.

"The fact that I haven't saved you," said Aria, "the fact that I can't . . . it doesn't mean you're going to . . ." Aria fumbled for the words. "It just means that's not what I'm here for. . . . I don't save lives," she said at last, wishing for the hundredth time she could. "I just do my best to make them better."

"Well, thanks," said Marco. "For making Gabby's better."

Aria smiled. The reading light beside the bed brightened. Marco yawned then, and Aria got to her feet.

"Good night, Marco," she whispered. "And good luck."

chāpter 29

GABBY

Marco went into surgery at 9:15 a.m.

Gabby knew because she'd memorized the time, and had then written it on her hand in case she forgot.

At 8:30 a.m., she and her mom had gotten to say their — not their *good-byes*, she couldn't think of it that way — *good-bye-for-now*s and *good luck*s. Marco had said he'd see them both after, and then he told Gabby she better not peek at his journal.

And then they'd rolled him away. Gabby had asked, as they were wheeling his bed into the hall, when the actual surgery would start, and one of the nurses had said 9:15 a.m.

It was now 3:38 p.m.

That meant Marco had been in surgery for six hours and twenty-three minutes.

Gabby watched the clock in the waiting room click to 3:39 p.m.

Six hours and twenty-four minutes.

Every time a door opened or closed she tensed, expecting a doctor to come out and tell them — she stopped herself. She didn't want to start thinking again about all the different things the doctor might tell them. She'd spent two hours — between 10:20 and 12:20 — doing that, and it had only made her panic worse. Her mom had let her skip school to be here, and she was beginning to wish she hadn't, because there was nothing to distract her. Nothing else to focus on. Not that she would have been able to focus on anything but this.

3:40 p.m.

She didn't realize she was humming until her mom reached over and took her hand. She didn't shush her, though, only squeezed her fingers.

The night before, Gabby had told Marco and her mom about getting the solo.

"Sing it for us," Marco had said.

"I don't know the song yet."

"Then sing me something," he'd said. "Anything."

Gabby ended up singing the song she'd auditioned with. Marco and her mom applauded, and Marco told her that next time he'd be in the audience and she'd be onstage. She told him to promise, and he said he'd do his best.

Marco, she thought, *you better do your best.*

3:45 p.m.

She felt a hand on her shoulder. Aria's. The post-op waiting room was family only, but Aria had promised she'd be there and Gabby knew she was, even though she couldn't see her. Seeing wasn't all there was to believing.

And then, finally, at 3:53 p.m, the doctor came in.

Gabby and her mom scrambled to their feet, still holding hands.

They waited for the news.

"The cancer was extensive," said the doctor, "And the operation was invasive. . . ." Gabby held her breath. "But Marco is quite a fighter."

Gabby's mom let out a cry of relief.

"He's got a long road to recovery, but if he does as well as he did today, he should make it through just fine."

Gabby's vision blurred from tears as her mom folded her into a hug. And then, over her mom's shoulder, Gabby noticed the waiting-room door open and then close, as if pushed by a breeze, or a small, invisible hand.

chapter 30

ARIA

Aria's shadow wouldn't stop fidgeting.

Even though she couldn't see it — couldn't see any part of herself — she could feel it moving restlessly around her feet. *Not yet*, she'd told it as the waiting-room clock ticked away the minutes. *Just a little longer*, she thought. And then the news had come, and Aria's heart had been filled with joy for Gabby and Marco and their mother, and she'd looked down at the place her shadow would be and thought, *Okay. Okay.*

She was halfway to the lobby, and visible again, when Gabby caught up to her and, without warning, threw her arms around her shoulders, nearly toppling her midstride. Aria had never been hugged like that before. A hug filled with happiness and hope.

"You were there," said Gabby.

Aria nodded. "I had to watch for smoke, remember?"

Gabby smiled, but then Aria started walking again, and the smile slid away.

"Where are you going?" Gabby asked.

Aria's heart sank as she made her way to the revolving doors. "I have to go, Gabby."

"But things are still so far from okay."

"I know," said Aria. "But they're on their way. You're on your way."

"To what?"

"To becoming a *who*," said Aria with a smile. "And that doesn't mean life is always going to be good or easy. It just means you're going to be a part of it."

Aria started toward the revolving doors again.

Gabby grabbed her arm. "Why do you have to go?" she asked. "You could stay in school. You could stay with me. We would find a way to —"

Aria shook her head sadly. Part of her really did wish she could stay. "No, Gabby. This is your life. I was just visiting."

She stepped through the revolving doors and out into the sun, the once-gray steps trailing vibrantly away from her.

"I can't do this without you," said Gabby beside her.

"Of course you can."

"Don't you want to know what happens next?"

Aria did, very much. She wanted to see Marco wake up, wanted to watch him recover, wanted to watch Gabby use her voice. But she knew in her chest she had to go. It was a pull stronger than gravity. She'd been here too long.

"You want to know what happens next?" said Aria. "You go to Marco's room, so you're there when he wakes up. He gets stronger every day and you get louder and he's there in the front row at your first choir concert. And you're there in the front row for his first soccer game, and you make sure that no matter what happens — no matter what happens — you don't lose your voice again. You don't forget who you are, because you, Gabby Torres, are amazing."

Tears shone in Gabby's eyes. "But will you come to the choir concert?" she asked. "Will you come back for that?"

Aria couldn't promise. She didn't know where she'd be. She wasn't entirely sure *who* she'd be, though she hoped she'd still be her. "I'll try," she said.

Gabby wrapped her arms around Aria one last time and then pulled away and went inside. Aria watched her go. There was nothing but air and hope wrapped around Gabby's shoulders.

Aria felt a cool kiss on her wrist. She looked down to see that a small blue feather charm had appeared on her bracelet. It made a sweet jingling sound when she moved her hand.

She smiled and wiped away a tear. And then she looked down at her shadow, and her heart thudded in her chest, because there, just above the shadow's shoulders and so faint they were barely visible, were the first hint of wings.

"I'm ready to go," said Aria. She snapped her fingers, and the girl-shaped shadow became a girl-shaped pool of light. And then she took a deep breath and vanished from sight.

chāpter 31

GABBY

Gabby forced herself not to look back.

She'd just come through the doors, a lump in her throat, when she heard two very familiar voices.

"No, his name is *Marco Torres*," Charlotte was saying at the front desk.

"I'm sorry," said the man behind it, "only family —"

"We just want to know if he's okay," said Sam.

"We just want to know what room he *would be in*," said Charlotte, "if he were out of surgery."

"Blink once for each floor," said Sam.

And then Charlotte turned and saw Gabby and said ohnevermind and then flung herself at her.

"You guys came," gasped Gabby.

"Duh," said Sam.

"Stupid school wouldn't let us out early," said Charlotte,

still smothering her. "And the stupid bus was late so we just hoofed it and —"

"Let her breathe," said Sam, and Charlotte pulled away.

"Sorry. How are you? I mean, how is he? I mean, how did it go?"

Gabby nodded gratefully. "He made it through the surgery."

Charlotte cheered loud enough that half the lobby turned in their direction.

"Sorry," she whispered, giving Gabby another squeeze.

"We were about to go room to room," said Sam. "What were you doing outside?"

Gabby looked back for the first time, past the revolving doors. There was no one there.

"I was just talking to Aria," she said.

"Who?" asked Charlotte.

Gabby's stomach twisted. "You know, *Aria*. Reddish hair. Colored shoelaces. Can't sing."

Charlotte shrugged. "Never heard of her."

Sam tipped his head. "Does she go to our school?"

Gabby's heart sank. How could they not remember her? Was that how Aria's magic worked?

"She's a friend," said Gabby. "I was just saying good-bye."

·   ·   ·

The auditorium was very, very full.

Grand Heights Middle School's first choir concert turned out to be a really big deal. Gabby stood backstage, trying not to freak out about the size of the audience. Charlotte squeezed her hand, and Sam said she could hold his soccer ball, if she thought that would help. And Charlotte said of course it wouldn't, and the two began to bicker playfully in a way that almost distracted Gabby from the stage and the lights and the waiting crowd.

Almost.

Marco couldn't come, not yet. It had been only a couple of weeks since his surgery, and even though he was getting stronger every day, it had been a hard road. But Gabby had put on a warm-up concert for him in the hospital the night before, and he promised to be at the next show. The doctors said he'd be strong enough to go home next week. *Home.* Maybe the house would finally start to feel like a home with him there.

Her mom was here, though, right in the front row.

"I think it's time, Gabby," said Charlotte gently.

"You ready?" asked Sam.

"No," said Gabby.

"Good!" said Charlotte. "True stars never are."

That made Gabby smile. Charlotte was always good at cheering her up. Like Aria had been. Sadness flickered through Gabby at the thought. Nobody seemed to remember Aria, not Charlotte or Sam or Mr. Robert or Ms. Riley, but Gabby did. Gabby would never forget.

She adjusted her outfit — a purple skirt with a white polo shirt and a glittery blue bow, the school colors — and took a breath. Then she stepped onto the stage with the rest of the choir.

The audience quieted, waiting. There were so many people. Gabby found her mother's face, glowing with pride. Gabby grinned and resisted the urge to wave.

Then Ms. Riley appeared. The choir teacher stood in front of the students, with her back to the audience, raising her hands to get their attention.

Gabby was secretly grateful to have something other than the crowd to focus on. Sam went over to the piano, set the soccer ball on the seat beside him, and began to play.

The moment the music started, Gabby's chest loosened. The choir sang three group numbers, and then it was her turn. The audience fell silent as she stepped up to the microphone and waited for Sam's cue. She could barely hear the first keys of the piano over her thudding pulse, but there it was, the beginning of the song. Gabby imagined Aria's hand resting on her shoulder as she closed her eyes and started to sing.

chapter 32

ARIA

If anyone had been standing outside the auditorium, they would have seen the shadow. It spread across the floor until it was roughly the size and shape of a twelve-year-old girl, and then it filled with light, and Aria rose out of it.

"Good shadow," she whispered.

She slipped into the auditorium under the roar of applause as the choir finished a group number. She lingered at the back of the crowd, invisible, and watched as a girl with long dark hair stepped forward, away from the group, and toward the microphone.

Gabby Torres smiled, closed her eyes, and began to sing.

As Aria listened, she could hear everything Gabby had been through, everything she felt, in those notes. Being invisible. Being lost. Being scared. New schools. Fresh starts. New friends. Aria. Henry. Marco.

And judging by the audience, who sat in rapt attention, they could hear it, too.

Aria held her breath the entire performance. When Gabby finished, and the room erupted into applause, Aria cheered with them, as loudly as she could. Gabby wouldn't be able to see her, but maybe she would hear her.

The applause faded away and Gabby rejoined the group, and the next number started. Aria knew it was time to go. But she wanted to do something, to show Gabby she'd been here, watching, listening.

So before she left, she turned Gabby's laces purple.

And then she turned away, the music following her as she crept out again, unnoticed. The shape at her feet filled with light, waiting, and Aria stepped through.

Don't miss Aria's next adventure in:

everyday angel #2:

Second Chances

The shadow took shape on the front steps of the school, between two manicured hedges and in front of a pair of rather imposing doors. At first the shadow was nothing more than a blot on the stairs, but soon it spread, spilling over the steps, growing to the size and shape of a twelve-year-old girl.

The shadow's skirt fluttered, and an instant later the whole shadow filled with light, and a form rose up out of it, until a girl stood there on the stairs, her shoes resting on top of the pool of light.

Aria blinked. She had no idea where she was, but she knew *who* she was — still herself — and for that she was thankful.

"Good shadow," she said, and the light under her feet went out.

She looked up at the stone mantle above the massive doors. It read:

WESTGATE PREPARATORY

. . . and in smaller print beneath it:

SCHOOL FOR GIRLS

Her blue charm bracelet still dangled from her wrist, a single silver feather hanging from the first loop. Two rings still hung empty, and as Aria gazed up at the front doors of the school, she felt a little thrill of excitement. Someone here, at this school, was waiting for her, even though they didn't know. Whoever it was, they would be marked for her, wreathed in smoke the same color as Aria's charm bracelet. And all Aria had to do was find them, and help them, and once she did, she'd be one step closer to earning her wings.

The school loomed, waiting, and she climbed the stairs toward the front doors. When she reached the landing at the top, she hesitated, and considered her laces. They were white, like the tennis shoes they were threaded through. Aria chewed her lip, and the laces turned a pretty purple. She smiled.

A little color couldn't hurt.

And with that, she pushed open the doors, and went in search of a girl with blue smoke.

She didn't get very far.

There was an office on the right, and she was only a few feet past the open door when a voice said, "Excuse me?" Aria paused, but didn't turn back, assuming the voice was speaking to someone else, but then it said, "Young lady?" and Aria realized there was no one else in the hall. She took a step backward into the doorway.

"Me?"

"Yes, you," said a woman at a desk. "What do you think you're doing?"

Aria looked around. The woman's tone made it clear she'd done something wrong, but she had no idea what.

"You can't just come waltzing in late," explained the woman in response to Aria's confused reaction. "That's an infraction."

"What's an infraction?" asked Aria.

"Being late."

"No, I mean, what *is* an infraction?"

The woman straightened the glasses on her nose, and cleared her throat. "An infraction means a broken rule." She pointed to a poster on the wall. It was covered in sentences that began with *NO*. No chewing gum. No cell phones. No tardiness . . . "Three infractions equal a detention."

Aria didn't know what a detention meant, either, but decided not to ask. "Sorry," she said. "I didn't know."

The woman looked over the glasses now, and squinted. "What grade are you in?"

"Seventh," said Aria, because she'd been in seventh grade back at Gabby's school. This school seemed very different, but hopefully the numbers stayed the same.

"What's your name?"

"Aria," said Aria.

The woman's gaze narrowed. "You don't go here."

Aria frowned. "Yes I do."

"Young lady, there are one hundred and seventy-three girls at Westgate Prep, and I know them all. I don't know you, so you don't go here."

"I'm new," explained Aria, glancing at the laptop behind the woman. "You can check," she added. She'd been able to imagine herself onto a class roster at Gabby's school. Surely she could imagine herself into a computer. At least she *hoped* she could.

The woman began typing away on the keyboard. "Last name?"

"Blue," said Aria, proud of herself for knowing now that a last name was a second name, and not the name you had before the one you have now.

The woman's fingers tapped furiously on the keyboard, and then stopped. "Huh," she said. "There you are."

Aria smiled. The lights in the office brightened slightly. The woman at the desk did not seem to notice.

"You're still late," said the woman, pushing a stack of pamphlets and papers across the desk toward Aria. "Surely you've already received all of this in the mail, and had time to read through our policies, do's and don'ts, etcetera. Normally, we'd have a student ambassador ready to welcome you, but I'm afraid I didn't know you were coming."

"Last minute," said Aria. "I didn't know, either."

"Yes, well, here's your schedule," said the woman, tapping the paper on top of the stack. "The seventh-grade girls are still at lunch, but it's almost over. Let me see if I can rustle up a sixth grader to show you where to go —"

"That's okay," said Aria brightly. "I'm sure I can find my way."

The woman hesitated. "Are you sure?"

Aria nodded. She had a student to find and a lot of school to cover, and she wanted to get going. A faint tug in her chest told her the girl was nearby.

"Very well," said the woman, already turning away. Aria hoisted the papers into her arms, and was nearly to the door when she said, "And, Miss Blue?"

"Yes, ma'am?"

The woman offered a small, begrudging smile. "Welcome to Westgate."

Four girls, one charm bracelet, and a little bit of luck . . .

Charmed Life
Caitlin's Lucky Charm
LISA SCHROED

Charmed Life
Mia's Golden Bird
LISA SCHROEDER

From the author of *It's Raining Cupcakes* comes a charming series about how anything is possible when you have great friends!